Kayla

I SWUNG around and stared at Dad with my mouth hanging open. He grinned at me and drained his beer. I looked back at Kayla.

I turned back to Dad. "She's your daughter?" I finally managed to say.

"I don't know why you stay in school, dumb as you are," Dad said, crushing the can. "Yeah, she's my daughter, and that makes her your sister."

I sat down too hard on one of our old folding chairs, and the leg snapped, dumping me on the floor. No one laughed, though. Now it was Kayla's turn to look shocked.

"You're my *brother*?" she said to me.

"Great. Both of 'em are stupid," Dad muttered, opening the fridge again.

● ● ●

OTHER SPEAK BOOKS

STETSON

S. L. ROTTMAN

speak

An Imprint of Penguin Group (USA) Inc.

SPEAK

Published by Penguin Group

Penguin Group (USA) Inc.,

345 Hudson Street, New York, New York 10014, U.S.A.

Penguin Books Ltd, 80 Strand, London WC2R ORL England

Penguin Books Australia Ltd, 250 Camberwell Road, Camberwell,

Victoria 3124, Australia

Penguin Books Canada Ltd, 10 Alcorn Avenue, Toronto, Ontario, Canada M4V 3B2

Penguin Books (N.Z.) Ltd, 182-190 Wairau Road, Auckland 10, New Zealand

First published in the United States of America by Viking, a division of Penguin
Putnam Books for Young Readers, 2002

Published by Speak, an imprint of Penguin Group (USA) Inc., 2003

3 5 7 9 10 8 6 4

THE LIBRARY OF CONGRESS HAS CATALOGED THE VIKING EDITION AS FOLLOWS:

Rottman, S.L.

Stetson / S. L. Rottman.

p. cm.

Summary: Seventeen-year-old Stetson meets the sister he never knew
he had, and together they try to make sense of their pasts.

[1. Brothers and sisters—Fiction. 2. Alcoholism—Fiction.
3. Automobile graveyards—Fiction. 4. High schools—Fiction. 5. Schools—Fiction.]

I. Title.

PZ7.R7534 Sr 2002 [Fic]—dc21 2001045545

ISBN 0-670-03542-4

Speak ISBN 0-14-250194-8

Printed in the United States of America

To AEW, APW, and KEW;
my world, my sunshine, and my starlight.

●

To the Widefield Gladiators of 1999–2000.
Thanks for letting me be part of your school year.

CHAPTER ONE

"SHE'S GONNA give a quiz. I just know it!"

"So what?" Julie flipped her long blond hair over her shoulder crossly.

"So what? So I'm this close to failing!" Chip held his thumb and forefinger apart about one inch. "If I fail, then I'm ineligible, and if I'm ineligible—" He broke off, aware for the first time that they were blocking my way into the classroom. He pulled Julie off to the side next to him, but I made no move to go in. Instead, I moved over with them.

"What do you want?" Julie demanded, wrinkling her pretty nose at me.

"What's it worth to you?" I asked Chip.

"What?"

"I can keep Ms. Pepper from giving a quiz today. What's it worth to you?"

They both stared at me in disbelief. To say that I was acquainted with either of them would have stretched the definition to the limit, even though we had gone to the same schools since kindergarten. They were in the cheerleader and football set, while I was, well, in a set all my own. I doubted they even knew my name.

"Excuse me, but we weren't talking to you!" Julie said, clearly offended that I would consider speaking to her.

I ignored her and waited for Chip's response.

"We don't know she's giving a quiz today," he began slowly.

"Haven't had one for a week now," I pointed out.

Julie turned in a huff and marched into the classroom.

Chip regarded me curiously. "They still haven't found all those mice you released last month, have they?"

I shook my head. The bell rang.

He sighed and turned into the classroom. Over his shoulder, he said, "Ten bucks."

I grinned as I followed him. This would be an easy ten.

"Chip, that's your second tardy. Stetson, it's your first," Ms. Pepper said, frowning at us as we sat down. Chip mumbled something that could have been an apology. I stayed quiet.

"Please get out your homework from last night and pass it in," she said, turning to the board.

There was a general shuffling and moaning as people either pulled out their work or realized they had forgotten to do it. She had given us the assignment as we left the room yesterday.

I don't do homework. If I get it done in class that's fine, but I don't take *anything* home with me. So I merely studied Ms. Pepper.

It was her first year teaching at Lincoln High, and it was probably her first year teaching ever. She was young, good-looking in a way, and she always dressed like she was still a teenager. Today she had on a pair of white pants and a yellow sweater.

The girls all liked her, because she was one of the cheerleader sponsors. The guys liked her because she often wore short skirts. She acted like she wanted to be our friend, and she always had a smile on her face.

Instead of lectures, she liked to give assignments and

then talk about them the next day. Most kids liked her because of that. I didn't. It was easier for me to learn from a lecture or notes. I can remember anything once I've written it down.

She put a few key words on the board, and then she quickly collected the homework. "Okay," she said, putting the stack of papers into a folder, "who wants to start?"

A row over and three seats ahead, Chip turned in his desk a little and grinned back at me. He flashed a ten-dollar bill in the palm of his hand and then slipped it into his pocket. He had written off the quiz. I hadn't.

I leaned back in my desk, content to wait and listen.

"Stetson?" Ms. Pepper smiled brightly at me. "What do you think?"

"I think you ought to back off," I said flatly, not even raising my eyes to look at her.

"Excuse me?" She blinked.

"You know I don't do homework, but every day you ask me questions about it. Just back off."

"Maybe you could try doing homework sometime," Ms. Pepper said in a voice that I'm sure she considered encouraging.

"Maybe you should just back off," I repeated, finally looking up.

Someone in the back of the class snickered. Ms. Pepper stared at me for a long minute. I never blinked and she finally looked away and asked someone else a question. I could see Chip shaking his head in front of me, but he didn't turn around.

I continued to slouch in my chair. Inside, though, I was

tense and nervous. I was still sure she was going to give a quiz. I wasn't mean to people very often, but I had decided how to get her to postpone the quiz. It wasn't that I disliked Ms. Pepper. Yeah, she irritated me, but I could handle that. I really needed that ten bucks. And I had just decided I wanted out of her class permanently.

Homework wasn't worth it for me. Any free time I had outside of school I spent working on my car, my art, or just working for cash. I supplemented my income by taking almost any dare I was offered. Last week it had been freeing mice because a girl didn't think it was fair for us to dissect them. Two weeks ago it had been pulling a fire drill in the middle of the pep assembly because a group of kids wanted to sneak out and get stoned. I did whatever was asked—for a price.

And I got caught only when I needed some time off from school.

The rest of the period dragged on. I was beginning to worry that maybe she wouldn't give a quiz and I would be out ten bucks. Finally, when there was only fifteen minutes left in class, Ms. Pepper stood up and closed her book.

"Now," she said, smiling her brightest, "if you would all please clear your desks for a quiz."

"What?" Julie exclaimed from the front of the room.

"You must be joking," the guy right behind her said.

"I never joke about things like this," Ms. Pepper said, still smiling cheerfully.

"We don't have enough time!"

"If we get started right now, we do. But the longer you whine about it, the longer it will take, and the greater the chance that you'll have to stay and work on it after the bell rings." The smile on Ms. Pepper's face never faltered.

I waited until Chip turned and looked at me. I wanted to make sure we still had a deal. He raised his eyebrows so high they disappeared under his bangs. It was still on.

"Oh, come on!" I said, slamming my hand down hard on my desk.

Everyone in the room stopped and stared at me.

Ms. Pepper waited a few seconds then said, "Do you have something to say, Stetson?"

"Just that you're pulling a load of crap here."

She shook her head at me. "I'm sorry you feel that way, but—"

"Quit taking it out on us."

"What?" The perma-smile faltered just a little. The whole class was watching me with a mixture of confusion and amusement.

"We all know why you've been in a bad mood these last two days. Why don't you deal with it and leave us alone?"

"I don't know what you're talking about, Stetson, but—"

"Just because you're on the rag doesn't mean you have to take it out on us."

Several of the guys snickered. Most of the girls turned around quickly, not looking at me. Ms. Pepper's cheeks got a little pink.

"Stetson, that's very rude, inconsiderate, and—" She stopped and turned around to her desk. She began scribbling furiously on a pad of paper. "Get your things," she snapped without looking up. "You're going to the office."

I stood up slowly, and picked up my notebook and pen. As I walked to the front of the classroom, I could almost feel the anger coming from all the girls in the class, and quite a few of the guys. I had, after all, picked on one of their favorite teachers and would be leaving them with not only a quiz but also a teacher in a bad mood. I glanced at the clock. Ten minutes left.

"You shouldn't have turned around to walk over here," I said.

Ms. Pepper struggled to keep her face blank. She held out the pass, trembling slightly, and said, "We'll talk about this later."

I went around her desk, getting very close to her. She took an involuntary step back and I took one forward. She held her ground this time, whether to try and save face or because the blackboard was just inches behind her, I don't know.

I dropped my voice so only she could hear, and said, "Wearing those pants today probably wasn't the best idea."

The angry flush in her cheeks was wiped away. She got as white as her pants. She looked over my shoulder and saw the class staring at her, the girls looking down at their desks and most of the guys still smirking. Turning, she nearly ran from the room. I had a hard time not laughing. I had only been looking for something that would offend her. I didn't think I'd be right about the timing.

While waiting for her to come back, I put my hand in my coat pocket, and looked at the stuff on her desk. The quiz was there, somewhere. Ah, there it was, half hidden by Ms. Pepper's overturned book. The class was silent and watching me. There was a sense of shock. They didn't know what I had said to her (although some of them might have had an idea), and they didn't know what I'd do if they said anything. I was unpredictable. It was just one of the reasons I was a loner.

The door was flung open violently, and the people in the closest desks jumped. Ms. Pepper stalked back in. Once again, her cheeks were red, but it wasn't because she had been laughing.

"Stetson," she practically shouted, "go to the office!"

I nodded. "I was just waiting to make sure you're okay," I said.

Her cheeks darkened even more. "Get out of my room!"

I walked slowly to the classroom door, and glanced at the clock. Seven minutes were left. She could probably give part of the quiz if she wanted to, but—

She walked quickly, not even glancing at me as we passed, and went directly to her desk. Trying to regain her normal calm composure, she said, "For the quiz you need a pen or a pencil, and remember to answer with complete—" she broke off with a scream and threw her book up in the air.

I walked over to Chip and he slipped me the ten.

Ms. Pepper backed away from her desk so fast she ran into the overhead projector cart, knocking it over. The crash and the breaking glass could barely be heard over her scream.

I opened the door and looked over my shoulder. "Nothing personal, Ms. Pepper," I said.

I don't know if she heard me. She never took her eyes off the dead mouse on her desk.

I stopped at the office on my way out. Mrs. Beard gave me a hateful look.

"What did you do this time, Stetson?"

I shrugged my shoulders. "He here?"

"Mr. Johnson is in a meeting. You'll have to wait in the In-School Suspension room."

Leaning over her desk just a little, I could see various times scribbled in for the rest of the day. I flipped the page over. Tomorrow was full, too, which was fine, because I needed a couple of days off.

"What are you doing?"

I flipped the page again. Finally, some empty space. "Just tell him I've suspended myself for the rest of today and tomorrow, and he and I can talk about it when I get back." I tapped a space on the page. "Eight o'clock should be just fine."

"Stetson," Mrs. Beard glared at me over her glasses, "it doesn't work that way."

"Sure it does. I'm saving us both lots of time and trouble." I turned to go.

"Stetson, if you leave now it will count as a truancy!"

"Whatever," I said over my shoulder. The door swung shut behind me, cutting off her reply.

CHAPTER TWO

"HEY, JASON?"

There was a metallic clang from the back of the shed. "Stet? That you?"

"Yeah, man." I worked my way back, being careful not to bump any of the piles that covered the floors and tables. I found Jason in the far corner, leaning into a washing machine.

"You know, you really ought to clean up around here. The place is starting to look like a dump."

Jason pulled his head out of the machine and rolled his eye at me. Today he was wearing his black POW/MIA patch. "You ever going to get tired of saying that?"

"Does it bug you?"

"You know it does."

"Then I think I'll keep saying it."

"You here to help or piss me off?"

I grinned. "You said you were going to have a lot of work this week."

"I got six totaled vehicles in today, two more coming in tomorrow, and you still ain't finished the four that came in last Friday."

"Well if you weren't so picky about how I strip and stash them—"

"If I weren't picky about how you strip and stash them, we'd both be out of business," Jason retorted. "If you're here to help, go get your happy little butt to work.

Otherwise, get the hell out of here."

"Yessir," I said, with a mock salute. Jason returned it with his middle finger.

I started out the door. "Why're you here today anyway?" Jason asked.

"You don't want to know," I said. I used to tell Jason about my pranks, but not anymore. He's the only one who actually wants me to stay in school.

He shook his head. "You're gonna end up on welfare or in the army if you're not careful," he said. "You know that, don't you?"

"Which would you recommend?" I asked.

"They both suck. The army would kick your ass into shape. Welfare will leave you sitting on a fat lazy one."

"Yeah, but welfare won't take any of my body parts."

He waved that away. Losing his eye in Vietnam wasn't an issue anymore. "At least the army might teach you some respect."

"Nah," I said. "I don't think anyone could teach me that."

"You might be surprised," Jason muttered, but his attention had already returned to the washing machine. His head and shoulders were disappearing back into it as I left.

I walked out into the salvage yard, past the rows and rows of metal shelves stacked with various parts. I had been working for Jason for almost seven years now, but it wasn't easy. Once I had accidentally put a lawn-mower motor in the row with the dishwasher motors, and he had threatened to fire me. Two days later, when I scratched a rearview mirror I was taking off a Lexus, he did. It took three weeks to convince him to let me have another chance. Jason kept the salvage yard more organized than most people keep their houses, and he only sold honest parts. He did good business.

The blue Ford I had half stripped was waiting for me. Once I had cleared it out and shelved all the salable parts, the electromagnet would lift the shell, take it to the crusher, and then set it in the pile of scrap metal. Next to the Ford were two Chevys and an Infiniti. I walked past them to see what the six newcomers were.

There was a new Bug and a classic one, and from the way they looked they could have been in the same accident. There was a pickup truck, another Ford, a Jeep Cherokee, and—

"I think those are the wheels you've been looking for," Jason said behind me, making me jump.

I walked over to the Civic. It had apparently been in a front-end collision. The hood, not large to begin with, was crumpled almost in half. Two large stars in the windshield and dark stains on the upholstery and dashboard made me wonder briefly if it had been a fatal accident. I quickly turned my attention back to the body of the car.

It had originally been gold, but was now covered mostly in primer. I dropped to my knees by the front tire. It was bald, but the spoke wire wheel was exactly what I had been looking for. It didn't appear to be bent.

I looked up at Jason. He was wiping his hands on a rag that was already covered with grease, but his smile was one of pure delight.

"All four?" I asked, barely daring to breathe.

He nodded. "Checked 'em as soon as it came in. They

all look good." I don't know what he saw on my face, but he said quietly, "They're yours, Stet. As soon as you finish stripping all these cars, that is," he added gruffly.

"All of them? I don't think so. I could buy 'em cheaper than that."

"Okay, okay. Two wheels for the work you do today, and two for what you get done tomorrow."

"But—"

"And you don't take 'em off the car till after you're done working tomorrow, neither."

I glared at him. He looked back calmly.

"Fine," I said. I had been waiting about eight months for wheels like this to come in. Another day hardly mattered.

"You'd better get to work," he said, turning around, "'Cause if you don't finish at least three of them cars by tomorrow, I won't consider the trade fair."

"Yessir," I said again. I didn't salute him this time, but it didn't stop him from flipping me off.

I went back to the Ford and really worked up a sweat for the next two hours. I figured I could get a good start on the Infiniti before I went home for the night. I was determined to get four cars done by tomorrow afternoon. That would be fair.

Jason busted my butt whenever I stepped out of line, but he also looked out for me. In addition to giving me parts for the work I did, he also slipped me some cash every week. The amount changed, depending on how many hours I had actually worked and what parts he had given me, but it was always enough to buy food for the week, and that was all that mattered.

● ● ●

I had first found the salvage yard when I was ten. I had wanted a dirt bike for Christmas, and even though I had known it wouldn't happen, I was somehow still crushed when the only thing I got was a used leather jacket. Looking back, I sometimes wonder why I had been so upset. I mean, at least I got *something* that year.

But I had left the trailer running, mad and hurt. I had run out of steam around the same time I reached the salvage yard. The gate was open, so I wandered in.

I had walked through what seemed like endless rows of junk before I came to what I now refer to as the "little stuff" row. In it were pieces of mopeds, fans, blenders, phones, and, of course, bikes.

There was one bike there that immediately caught my attention. It was a dark blue Huffy. I was so excited when I saw it, that I actually started to climb on it before I realized that one of the handlebars was missing and the rear wheel was bent at an impossible angle.

"Hey, kid, get off that bike!"

I jumped and tried to get off, but I got tangled up instead and the bike and I went over in a clatter.

A guy came stomping up to me, his bright eye glaring, the other one mercifully hidden by a black pirate's patch.

"What're you doing here?"

"I just . . . saw the . . . wanted to try . . ." I began to splutter.

"What?" he yelled.

"I . . . I . . ." and the tears I thought I had left at my father's trailer began to fall again.

"Oh, get up," Jason said crossly. "I ain't gonna bite ya or beat ya. Just get outta here."

I struggled to stand, but I was still tangled up with the bike.

With a disgusted sigh, he reached over and pulled the bike and me up at the same time. "Now go on. Get."

I hesitated. He had scared me, but somehow I could sense he wasn't mean. "What are you gonna do with it?"

"Wait for someone to buy it," He grunted as he put the bike back with the rest of them.

"But it's broke!"

"Yeah, but someone could fix it again."

I looked at him for a second before I said, "How much?"

He stopped and looked at me again. "It's Christmas," he said finally. "I ain't open right now."

"I ain't got money right now," I said. "How much?"

"Why aren't you home?"

I shrugged.

He sighed and looked up at the heavy gray sky for a second, then he looked back at me. "You know how to fix it?"

"No," I said. "But I bet I can figure it out."

"You come back after school starts," he said. "I'll show you how to fix it."

"How much?"

"We'll talk about it later. Now get out of here."

"How much?" I repeated. My father never took charity.

"I said later! And if you don't leave right now, I'll never let you back in the yard! Now get!" he had yelled.

I got.

Ten days later, when school started, I had gone back. He grinned when he saw me. He had traded his black eye patch for a green and yellow one. I soon learned that the color of his patch reflected his mood.

"Serious about that bike, huh?"

I nodded, shifting from one foot to the other.

"Well, come on then." He turned and started down one of the rows.

"How much?" I asked. My pockets were full of change. I had every penny I could find in the house, even digging under the sofa cushions, but in my heart I didn't believe it would be enough.

Jason had sighed and turned back to look at me. "Still stuck on that, are ya?"

I didn't say anything, just met his one-eyed stare and waited.

"Here's what I had in mind," he said, smiling just a little. "I'll teach you how to fix a bike. You fix two bikes for me, and you can keep one of them."

"Really?" I couldn't believe he'd just give me a bike like that. Of course, I had no idea what I was getting myself into.

I spent the next two weeks after school learning the difference between a Phillips and a standard screwdriver, what a ratchet wrench was good for, the metric sizes, how to use pliers and wire cutters, and everything else my father had never taught me. Then I spent the following week taking a bike apart and putting it back together again. The week after that, I finally fixed the two bikes.

I hung out around the yard a lot after that. Over the summer, I learned how to rebuild lawn mowers. The following year, it was washers and dryers. Then Jason started me in on the cars. That's when he actually began scheduling my time and paying me.

And through it all, Jason was there, yelling when I screwed up, praising when I got it right, asking me questions and usually answering mine.

● ● ●

After I finished stripping the blue Ford, I picked up my toolbox and moved to the Infiniti. I glanced at the Civic, but refused to give in to temptation.

The Infinity's passenger side had taken the brunt of the impact. The passenger seat was a mess, but the driver's was still in decent condition, with only one small tear in the leather. I carefully pulled it out. I pulled the passenger seat out, too, and set it to one side. Jason wouldn't sell it, but it would be a good chair to take breaks on.

With the seats out, it was easier to get to the dashboard and accessories. There was a really nice Pioneer CD player, and I pulled it out, being careful not to cut any wires. The speakers, strangely enough, were just the regular factory-installed ones. But I was just as careful pulling them out, because you never could tell who might buy them.

"You ain't done yet?" Jason barked.

I had kind of lost myself while working the car. I tried to sit up too quickly and slammed my head into the dashboard.

"Ow! Bet that hurt," Jason chuckled, sitting down on the driver's seat and clinking two bottles.

I crawled out, sat on the passenger seat, and looked around. "What time is it?"

"Past quittin' time, that's for sure," Jason said, handing me a soda.

"Thanks, man," I said, twisting the bottle open and taking a long drink. I had been working for hours without a break.

"I noticed the wheels are still on that Civic."

"You told me not to touch them."

"Thought you might decide to take 'em off anyway."

"Thought about it," I confessed.

"What'cha got to work on tonight?"

I shrugged. "Not much."

"Gonna start paintin' tonight?"

"Nah, I'm gonna give it one more once over with the buffer."

"Son, you're gonna sand right through the metal if you're not careful."

"I *am* careful! I just want to make sure it's right before I paint."

"You still haven't figured out what to put on it, have you?"

"No," I grumbled.

Jason laughed and took another pull on his beer.

We sat in silence for a few moments, just enjoying the quiet breeze after a long day's work. Mentally I created and rejected designs for my Civic.

"You said you can work tomorrow?"

I nodded, sipping the soda.

"How about this weekend?"

"Sure," I said. "Don't I always?"

"I didn't know if you were gonna try to do the first coat this weekend. It'll take a while to set, you know."

"I know. I thought I'd wait till next week."

"And miss more school?" Jason raised his eyebrows at me.

"Yeah, I know. But that way Dad'll be at work. Don't have to worry about him opening the shed door in the middle of the day and letting all the dust and bugs in."

"You gotta pass all your classes if you're gonna graduate this spring."

"I will. I haven't missed too much this semester."

Jason grunted, but just asked, "Can you run the show this weekend?"

"What do you mean?"

"I got to go up to the city this weekend. Instead of closing the yard, I thought I'd let you run it."

"You're gonna leave a delinquent like me in charge?"

He grimaced and shifted in his seat. "You don't need to remind me that it ain't a great idea."

I grinned. "I'll be here."

"Good." He took a last pull on his beer and then stood up. "Well, then, we'd better get busy."

"Thought you said it was past quittin' time."

"Still got a lot to do."

"Like what?"

"Getting those wheels off, for one."

"I thought you wanted me to finish the other cars first."

He shrugged. "Might as well give you something productive to do tonight, instead of buffing that poor car one more time."

I laughed.

He helped me pull off all four wheels, and then carry them to the shed.

"You want to use the wheelbarrow again?"

"Nah. I'll just take two home tonight and get the other two tomorrow."

"You sure?"

"Yeah."

He spent about ten minutes going over how to enter things in the book and how to run the register. When he started repeating things for the third time, I interrupted him.

"Jason, I ain't new here. I know what I'm doing."

"Yeah, I know, but you've never been the boss."

"I can handle it."

"You sure?"

I grinned. "You wouldn't have asked me if you didn't think I could do it."

"Good point." He closed the register and locked it. I picked up the two wheels. "How 'bout I give you a ride home and you take all four?"

I shook my head. "Thanks, but this will be all right."

"You sure?"

"Yeah." He lived in the opposite direction from my house. We started walking toward the front door. "What are you going into the city for?"

"Just got some errands to run."

"They can't wait till Sunday?" The yard was only open from noon to four on Sundays.

"You trying to bail on me already?" He locked the door behind us.

"No, just trying to help out. I know you hate leaving the yard in someone else's hands."

"Not yours," he said, clapping a hand on my shoulder. "And I've got to do this stuff this weekend."

"What stuff?"

"If I wanted you to know, I'da told you about it." He opened his car door. "You sure you don't want a ride?"

I shook my head again and started walking toward the

gate. "I'll get the chain after you pull out," I said. "See you tomorrow mornin'."

"Okay," he said, sliding his big frame awkwardly behind the steering wheel of his '68 Bug. "See you tomorrow." He pulled the door shut, started the engine, and drove past me slowly, but still kicked up a lot of dust and gravel.

I walked through the gates and set the wheels down on the other side. Quickly I pulled the metal gates together and looped the chain through both of them twice before snapping the padlock shut. Then I turned back for my long walk home.

The wheels were heavy, and I knew I'd have to stop and rest several times on my two-mile walk, but I was in no hurry.

My mother left when I was three and a half. I don't miss her now because I don't really even remember her. When I was little I used to try to imagine what she was like, but eventually I gave up. I couldn't picture anyone who would stay with my father, even for just three years.

Every once in a while, I get a kind of memory flash: a laughing face, a bit of a nursery song, a soothing hush and a light touch. But the images are all vague. She left us in the double-wide trailer we're still living in. If she ever wanted to, she could find us.

My father works at the mill from eight to five Monday through Friday. From five to midnight or close, he sits on a barstool at MacGregor's Bar. He's gotten so many DUIs that he can't get his license back for another ten years. That wouldn't stop him from driving, but since he can't afford to buy a car and he totaled the last one, the only time he drives now is when one of his buddies is drunker than he is.

The first phrase that comes to mind when I think about my father is "drunken slob." He's got a huge beer gut, I'm not sure how often he bathes each week, and if I didn't do the dishes at least once in a while, he'd probably just eat off the dirty ones. It wasn't always this way. Things were good before Mom left.

After she left, he did his best to take care of me. In fact, for a while he treated me better than he had before she left. I have memories of Dad as a laughing and caring person, but each year I got taller, his love got smaller. It was a gradual decline that bottomed out when I got to junior high. I came home from my first day and he took me to MacGregor's to celebrate. He got trashed, and puked on me as I was helping him home. We got in a fight about it the next day, and I don't think he's done or said anything positive since. The thing we argue about the most right now is school.

I want to finish school.

My father dropped out when he was sixteen and a sophomore. The fact that I'm seventeen and still in school bugs him to no end. He's always complaining about the fact that I'm only working part time. Dad can't understand why I stay in school and work part time at the salvage yard instead of full time with him at the mill. And he doesn't realize that the more he nags me, the more determined I become.

For a while there, I thought he was upset because he wanted me bringing more money home, but the snide comments have started coming in more and more lately, so

I don't think money's the issue. I think he's mad that I'm actually going to graduate.

The other thing he's upset about right now is my car. I bought it two years ago, and I spend every spare minute and penny I can working on it. It's just a 1980 Honda Civic, but I've reconstructed nearly all of it. What drives Dad nuts is that I won't drive it and I won't let him touch it.

The shortest route from the salvage yard to the trailer park passes MacGregor's. I always walk past it as fast as I can. I don't want to see my father, but more importantly, I don't want to see any of my old friends.

"Stet!"

Startled, I turned around. I had been so wrapped up in my thinking, I hadn't noticed Tony's old El Camino pulling into the lot. I started to say hi and nothing came out. It always spooks me when I start thinking about someone and then they appear, as if my thoughts called them.

I cleared my throat and tried again. "Hey, Tony!" I managed to call. I set the wheels down by my feet and waited while he parked.

There were six of us who grew up in the trailer park together. We played tag and hide-and-go-seek as kids, and then we collected baseball cards for a while. When we got to junior high, we quit trick-or-treating and started smashing pumpkins. We started skipping school and smoking. We all bitched about our parents and the stupid one-horse town we lived in, and we all agreed we'd find a way to beat the system and get out.

When we got to high school, all of us went out for the football team, thinking we'd be great athletes and get out of town that way. Between the cigarettes and the fact that none of us had ever played the game before, only two of us made the team. Tony quit when he found out he and I were the only ones who made it. I quit two weeks later. High school ball didn't pay bills.

One by one the others dropped out and went to work for the mill full time. Tony held on the longest. He finally quit last year.

"Man, how are you?" he exclaimed, jumping out of the El Camino and slamming the door. "It's been years!"

"Yeah, it's been forever," I agreed. I had seen Tony just this summer at his wedding. "How's the baby?"

"She's fine," he said, grinning. It was a big smile, but it didn't quite reach his eyes. "She keeps us busy, though, that's for sure."

I nodded, but wondered why he always stopped at the bar if the baby kept him so busy. Aloud I said, "I'm sure all the work's worth it, though."

"Hey, why don't you come in? We'll have a couple of beers and talk about stuff."

If you work at the mill, you get served at MacGregor's, no matter how old you are. Everyone there knew me 'cause of my old man. I had been going in to get him for one thing or another since I was seven.

"Thanks, man," I said, shaking my head. "But not this time. Maybe next."

He nodded as if that's what he had expected. "How's school? You still hanging in there?"

"By my fingernails."

"Yeah, right." Tony knew I could get by. "The kids still buying your shirts?"

"Not quite so much," I lied.

"Bummer, man. I thought you might get somewhere with that."

When I was eight, Dad bought me new school clothes. I pitched a fit because all he had gotten me was three pairs of jeans and three multi-packs of plain white T-shirts. A month later, I had decorated all of the shirts with markers, and sold four of them to kids in my class.

By the time I was in junior high, I had saved enough to buy an airbrush. Now I usually sell about six a month, and so far I had already been approached by two clubs to design shirts for them.

"You still putting that car together?"

"Yeah."

"I woulda thought you'd be done by now."

I shrugged. "Guess I just work slow."

Tony grinned again, but it was a hard grin. "You mean you don't settle for a half-assed job to just get it done."

I bent down to pick up the wheels. "If that's the case, then I'd better get to work," I said, starting to walk away.

"Tell your dad I hope he feels better."

I stopped and turned back around. "What do you mean?"

"He called in sick today."

"He did?"

"Yeah."

"That's strange," I said, mostly to myself.

"Well, I'll tell Vicky I saw you. She still asks about you once in a while." Vicky had dated almost all of the guys in our little group. Although she and I had only gone out for a few weeks, she had once told me I was the one she felt closest to. I don't know why. I didn't talk to her any more than I talked to anyone else. I just listened.

I nodded as I crossed the parking lot. "Tell her I said hello!" I called over my shoulder. Tony was already disappearing into the bar.

As I walked into the trailer park, I tried to remember the last time Dad had stayed home from work. I think it was the morning after he got that last DUI. He had been drunk enough when they pulled him over, but after they gave him the ticket he came home and drank a bottle of vodka. He didn't move out of the bathroom the next day.

I walked around our double-wide to the shed in the back where I kept my car. I almost walked into John Stevens's truck. It was parked between the shed and the trailer. Dad must have borrowed it for something.

After setting the wheels down and opening the padlock on the shed, I hesitated. What I really wanted to do was take the wheels inside and get to work. A tiny part of me felt like I should go check on Dad, make sure he was okay. I couldn't seem to quit feeling the need to take care of him, even though he had stopped taking care of me a long time ago.

One of the trailer's back windows popped open.

"Stetson! Get your ass in here!" Dad bellowed.

I sighed. I should have just gone right in the shed. He wouldn't have even known I was home.

"Stetson!" He yelled again. He knew I hated my full name.

"Coming!"

I set the wheels just inside the door, locked the padlock, and headed toward the trailer.

CHAPTER THREE

I OPENED the front door and stopped in surprise. The curtains were almost always drawn shut. Today they were wide open, and the room that was usually dark, dirty, and dusty was bright and somewhat clean. In fact, the setting sun was almost causing a glare off Dad's old rodeo trophies.

Seeing Dad with his big beer belly, scrawny arms, and thin graying hair, it's hard to imagine him as the bull-riding champ he once was. He claims he gave up the sport to stay home with his family, but I've always had a sneaking suspicion that the chunk of his cheek he lost to a bull's horn had something to do with it too.

Holding my hand up to shield my eyes, I blinked for a moment, blinded by the glare. "Hello?"

"Hey." I heard a beer cracking open in the kitchen.

"What are you doing here?"

"Last time I checked, I'm the one who pays the rent here."

"What's up? Why aren't you at MacGregor's?"

"Who's MacGregor?"

I stepped farther into the room, still blinking from the glare. There was a girl sitting on our sofa. She looked about my age and was sitting at the very edge of the cushions, like she wasn't sure she should be sitting at all. Her tight T-shirt stopped a good four inches above her equally tight miniskirt. There were two suitcases at her feet.

"Who are you?"

"I'm Kayla. Who are you?" She may have looked nervous on the edge of the couch, but her voice was harsh. So were her dark eyes. She had long black hair, and olive-colored skin like mine.

"I'm Stet," I said.

"Stet?"

"Stetson," my father corrected. I rolled my eyes.

"Hi, Stet," Kayla said coolly.

"Why are you here?"

"My mother died last week. No one else would take me."

"Your mother . . . I'm sorry." I shook my head, trying to make sense of what was happening. Dad was leaning against the kitchen counter, smirking at both of us, enjoying the show. "So why are you *here*?" I repeated.

"My mom's friend dug up your phone number and called last night."

I stared at her expectantly, waiting for the rest of the story, waiting to find out how she was connected to us.

Kayla gave an exasperated sigh. "So Dad came and got me this morning and brought me back here."

I swung around and stared at Dad with my mouth hanging open. He grinned at me and drained his beer. I looked back at Kayla, then I turned back to Dad. "She's your daughter?" I finally managed to say.

"I don't know why you stay in school, dumb as you are," Dad said, crushing the can. "Yeah, she's my daughter, and that makes her your sister."

I sat down too hard on one of our old folding chairs, and the leg snapped, dumping me on the floor. No one laughed, though. Now it was Kayla's turn to look shocked.

"You're my *brother*?" she said to me.

"Great. Both of 'em are stupid," Dad muttered, opening the fridge again.

"I'm not stupid!" Kayla snapped. "But you haven't said anything about him all day!"

"That's nothing," I said from the floor. "He hasn't said anything about you, ever."

"That's because I didn't know about her," Dad said. He came into the living room, belched, and flopped onto the couch. He nodded in my direction. "Hey, smart boy, that looks really comfortable."

"It is, thanks," I said. I had been just about to get up, but now I simply shifted and pulled the chair leg out from under me. "There's not much difference between sitting on the floor and that old sofa anyway."

"Any time you want to leave, I'm sure you're smart enough to find the door," he said mildly. He meant it, though. He always did. The only reason he let me stay was for the tax write-off, and as he had told me for the last two years, that really wasn't much incentive any more.

Kayla had shrunk back into the other corner of the couch, as far away from Dad as she could get.

My mind was still spinning. Dad had never told me why Mom left. It had been a puzzle my brain still tried to solve late at night when I wasn't looking.

"Mom was pregnant when she left? I guess back then you weren't spending all your time being a barfly. MacGregor's must not have been built yet, huh?"

He turned and flung the beer can at me. I ducked and it missed, but I realized that I must have struck a nerve—the can wasn't empty yet.

"So what happened?"

He glared at me. "She saw what a lousy brat you were turning into, and decided she didn't want you around to rub off on the next baby!"

I turned to Kayla. My mother left a month before my third birthday. "How old are you?"

"Fourteen."

"You look a lot older."

"It's all the makeup," Dad said. "Your mother thought she could raise a kid better on her own, but all she succeeded in doing was raising a slut."

Even from across the room I could see Kayla literally bite down on whatever she was about to say. Her face darkened a little and she shrank even farther into the sofa, pulling self-consciously at her tight shirt.

"Why didn't you tell me?" I was staring at Kayla but talking to Dad.

"I told you, moron, I didn't know. The first I heard about her was when I got called last night."

"So why didn't you tell me last night? I would have gone with you to get her."

"I didn't think you'd want to miss any of your precious school time," he sneered at me.

Quietly I said, "It would have been nice to at least see my mother's grave. Or meet some of her family." Dad had never mentioned any relatives, from his side of the family or from hers.

"Believe me, you didn't miss nothin'."

I glanced over at Kayla and saw her quickly wipe her face with the back of her hand. She was trying to be hard, but he was getting to her.

"I'm sorry about your—our—mother," I said awkwardly. She just nodded.

"I'm the one you should be sorry for," Dad said. "After all, now she's left me stuck with two of you."

It was Dad's idea of a joke. I had never bothered to tell him that he wasn't funny.

"You shut up!" Kayla suddenly screamed, jumping up off the couch. "You shut up about my mother! You didn't know her. You're just some stupid white trailer trash and my mother was too good for you! You're not even good enough to wash her underwear! You can't possibly be my father."

Dad hauled himself to his feet. "*You*'re the one who's gonna sit down and shut up, Missy. Else I'll be teaching you the manners your mother didn't."

My father may have scrawny arms and a big beer gut, but he's still almost six foot four. Kayla wasn't more than five foot five. She backed up quickly around the end of the couch.

I felt myself tensing all over, ready to jump up and get between them. Dad hadn't raised his hand to me for more than six years, but that didn't mean he wouldn't try to make an impression on her.

"I'm leaving!" she shouted. "There's no way I'm gonna stay in this dump!"

Dad laughed his harsh, angry laugh. "Listen, Stetson! You finally got an ally."

"You can't make me stay," Kayla began.

"I wouldn't try," Dad said flatly. "I've been trying to get Stetson to leave for a couple of years. But there's one thing you're forgetting, *daughter*." His voice practically dripped sarcasm.

Kayla looked at him warily.

"No one else wanted you."

She flinched as if she had been hit. "That's not true," she whispered.

"Why do you think Brandi called me?"

"The will. It had something to do with Mom's will. She left me in your custody."

Dad waved his hand. "If they wanted you, they'd fight it. After all, I've never even laid eyes on you before. Your grandmother and Brandi have been around you since you were just a little snot. They could get custody. If they *wanted* it." He finished harshly.

I felt bad for Kayla, but I didn't know how to stop this kind of abuse. She looked around wild-eyed, panicked and terrified. I didn't blame her.

Dad hitched up his pants. "You can go or you can stay. You saw how we came into town, so I'm sure you can find your way back out again. But I've got to go return John's truck, and although your brother has a car in the shed, it's as useless as he is. He's been working on it for years and it still doesn't run. So if you go, it'll be on your two feet."

"I hate you," Kayla muttered.

"You ain't known me long enough to hate me. Give it a few days, then you can mean it when you say it." He walked toward the front door.

I could see the tears glittering in Kayla's eyes, but she didn't let them fall.

"Stetson'll take you to school tomorrow."

"I won't go."

"You'll go," Dad said as he pulled on his beat-up denim jacket. "The day you turn sixteen or get married you can quit if you want to. But I'm not going to have the cops on my case 'cause you're screwing around, so you'll go to school."

"Just not tomorrow," I said.

"What?" Dad said, turning toward me.

"Just not tomorrow," I repeated, "unless you're gonna take her."

"Why should I have to take her when you're going?"

I was tempted to tell him he should take her simply because he's her father, but all I said was, "I'm suspended."

"What'd you do this time?"

Shrugging, I said, "Nothing."

"Stetson, what did you do?"

"Don't go putting on a concerned father act for her," I snapped. "You don't care if I go to school or not."

"He couldn't act like a concerned father if he tried," Kayla said from behind the couch.

Dad glanced at her in surprise and laughed. "Well, at least you're not entirely stupid." He opened the front door and it banged shut behind him.

I stood up, wincing.

"Floor's not really that comfortable, is it?"

"Not really."

"Is there a phone book?"

"Why?"

"Not that it's any of your business, but I want to call a cab and get out of here."

"I don't think that's such a great idea."

"You can't play a concerned brother any better than that scum can play a concerned father," she said, "so don't even try. I'd like to call a cab, but if you're not gonna help me do that, I'll just walk." She came back around the couch to get her bags.

"Now you *are* being stupid," I said. "You don't even have a place to go. Plus, it's at least a three-mile walk into town, and you pass two roadside bars along the way. It's no place for you to be walking alone in the dark, especially dressed like that."

"There's nothing wrong with what I'm wearing!" she yelled. A couple of tears escaped from her eyes.

I let it go. Dad had already given her too much grief. "Look, it's been a rough day for both of us. I'll show you where you can sleep tonight, and maybe you can figure something out in the morning."

Kayla stared at me suspiciously for a few moments before she sniffled and said, "Okay."

I led her down the short hall to the room on the left and opened the door.

She peered in, then said, "This is your room."

"Yeah."

"Where are you going to sleep?"

"I'll take the sofa," I said.

She nodded but didn't say anything as she walked past me and shut the door.

CHAPTER FOUR

THE EARLY-morning light woke me. The shed didn't have any windows, but there were plenty of cracks that let the sun shine in. I had been collecting large sheets of plastic for a while now. When it came time to paint, I would use them to cover the walls and make it as airtight as I could. You can't have stuff blowing around when you paint a car, or it will become a permanent part of the vehicle. Plus, it will look bad. And my car was going to be perfect.

I sat up slowly and adjusted the bucket seat into a more comfortable position. When fully reclined, the seats were almost as comfortable as my bed.

After Kayla had shut me out of my room, I had come out here and worked. I had buffed the car one more time, doing that first so it wouldn't keep Kayla awake. Then I put the two wheels on the front.

Jason was the only one who knew that my car ran perfectly. I had driven her six times so far, always in the early hours of the morning, testing the engine as I had rebuilt it. The rest of the time I just let her idle in the shed, for at least ten minutes a night. There was nothing better than the sound of her purr. I could easily have been driving to school and around town, but I had decided to wait until she was done. Her faded, buffed, and mismatched panels weren't fit to be seen.

I climbed out of the car and stretched, reaching up and almost touching the low ceiling. I had gotten most of

Dad's height. Mom must have been short, like Kayla.

All the hard work last night hadn't been able to drive Mom and Kayla from my mind. Even my few hours of sleep were full of them.

When I was in second grade, I had come home with a question for our science unit. I was supposed to look at family history about hair and eye color. Since I knew nothing about either family, I had asked Dad for help. After looking at it for a minute, he tore it up, said it was a stupid assignment, and then went to the bar. We never spoke about it again.

It was a topic that not even my wandering thoughts had wanted to touch very often. Every possible reason for her leaving had unpleasant results. To finally learn that she had left because she was pregnant was like losing her all over again. If she had loved the unborn baby that much, why hadn't she loved me enough to take me along? If she couldn't do that right away, why hadn't she ever come back, or even called to talk to me?

"I thought you were gonna sleep on the couch."

I jumped, and hated myself for doing it. "Didn't anyone teach you to knock?"

Kayla gave me a half-smile and came the rest of the way into the shed. "So this is the car, huh?" She ran a finger lightly along the fender. "Not much to look at."

"Not yet," I said stiffly.

"But it will be?" Her voice was falsely sweet. It looked like she had more makeup and less skirt on than last night.

Instead of answering her, I rubbed my face vigorously, trying to finish waking up. I ran my tongue over my teeth and grimaced. I needed my toothbrush, badly.

"You should gargle. Here," she said, holding out a beer can.

I raised my eyebrows at her. "What are you doing with that?"

She shrugged. "Getting a head start on Happy Hour." She took a sip, her eyes trying to look innocent over the rim.

"It's not even eight in the morning!"

"So?"

"You're too young to be drinking."

"You're not my father."

"I'm your brother."

"As of last night."

"That's not my fault, and that's not the point."

She tossed her hair. "It helps me get started in the morning."

I stared. "You usually start the day drinking?"

Kayla almost looked self-conscious.

"You know that's a sign that you're an alcoholic," I continued.

"Please," she said. "I don't need a lecture. I've had a rotten week, and last night just really sucked. I think the least I deserve right now is a drink. You probably need one just as much." She held the can out again.

"No thanks."

"Come on! I don't want to drink alone."

"So quit drinking!" I retorted.

"You're not any fun," she pouted.

"I don't drink."

Now she laughed. "Get serious."

"I am."

Uncertain, she pulled the can back to her. "Why not?"

I had been asked that many times, but had never bothered to answer it. I surprised myself now by saying, "You've met our father."

"Yeah. And?"

"I'm not gonna be him."

She started to laugh but stopped when she realized I was serious. "You won't become Dad just from a drink or two."

I shrugged. I could see that there was no point talking to her right now, in telling her about the times I had had a drink or two, or four, or six; finding myself unable to stop until I blacked out.

"Is Dad inside?"

"His truck's gone."

"That wasn't his truck. He doesn't have a car."

"Oh," Kayla said, thinking that over. "Well, I didn't hear him inside, but I don't know for sure," she said, tipping the beer can up and taking a few swallows. "Don't really care, either." She belched.

I sighed. "Great. Well, give me a few minutes to shower and get ready."

"For what?"

"To take you to school."

"Don't worry about it."

I leaned against my car. "Are you gonna go stay with someone else?"

"I haven't decided what I'm doing yet," she said, setting the empty can on the hood.

I reached across and knocked the can off so quickly she jumped.

"Hey!" she exclaimed.

I ignored her and started toward the shed door. "You might as well be in class while you're deciding what you're gonna do."

"You're trying to act like my father again."

I bit down a bitter laugh. "I'm not acting *anything* like your father," I said as I stepped outside. "Come on. Let's go."

"I'd rather wait out here," she said.

"Too bad," I said flatly. "Move it."

She did, but slowly. As soon as she was out of the shed, I shut the door and fastened the padlock.

"You're really worried about someone taking that half-done car?"

There was no reason to answer that, so I didn't.

Inside the trailer, I checked to see if Dad was still there. I really didn't want to take Kayla to school. His filthy bedroom was empty. I sighed and went to my room to get a change of clothes.

At the door, I stopped in shock. I don't own much, so it's pretty easy to keep my room neat. Kayla had only brought the two suitcases, but somehow she had managed to make my room look almost as trashed as Dad's. Her clothes were everywhere, the sheets were falling off my bed, she had set her makeup on my table and knocked most of my stuff off of it onto the floor, and I couldn't believe how many shoes were flung around the floor.

I heard a can popping open, and I turned my head to look down the hall. From the kitchen, Kayla raised another beer at me and smiled.

I shook my head, found some clothes, and took them to the bathroom.

After showering and brushing my teeth, I felt a little better, but not much. The last thing I wanted to do today was go to school. I had never been worried about keeping the family name clean, so Kayla was going to be starting with some teachers who wouldn't like her just because of me. Plus, I wasn't convinced she wouldn't be adding her own horror stories.

She was stretched out on the couch, watching some trashy talk show. I went into the kitchen, trying to ignore the TV as people screamed at each other about who had cheated on who with who first.

Opening the fridge, I sighed. The eggs and milk I had bought last week were gone, and so was the orange juice. All that was left was half a bottle of ketchup, a jar of pickles, a stick of butter, and four six-packs of beer. Dad usually only kept two in the fridge at a time, so I guessed Kayla had found the supply in the closet and moved it.

I went to the cupboard and looked for the loaf of bread. It was gone. I swore under my breath and turned to the box of cereal. It was empty. The second one was too. It really pissed me off that Dad always left the empty boxes in there. I turned to the other cupboard and found a box of cheese crackers and a bag of corn chips. I chose the chips, figuring they were at least sort of related to corn flakes.

I was just throwing the bag into the trash when Kayla came into the kitchen. She tossed her can into the trash and opened the fridge. When she came out with another beer in her hand, I stopped her.

"Put it back and go brush your teeth."

"Why?"

"So we can get you to school."

She groaned and rolled her eyes at me. "You can't be serious."

"I am."

Suddenly she gave a mischievous grin. "We'll go as soon as I'm done with this," she said, cracking it open.

I grabbed it out of her hand before it got to her mouth, and then upended it over the sink.

"Hey!" she squealed. "That's perfectly good beer you're wasting!"

"And this is perfectly good time you're wasting. I don't have all day for this. Go brush your teeth."

She pouted, sticking her lower lip out and looking up at me through her eyelashes. "I just want one more," she said, swaying lightly back and forth.

"Is that how you usually get what you want? You'll have to learn another way, because Dad and I aren't gonna care about your sad eyes."

Those sad eyes flashed angrily. She tossed her hair and flounced out of the kitchen. I had never actually seen someone flounce before, but she did. She flounced right over to the couch and flopped down.

"I mean it, Kayla. Go brush your teeth."

"I'm not going and you can't make me."

I leaned across the counter and looked at her. "You don't want to see me try."

She glared at me for a second but then dropped her eyes and muttered, "There's no point in going 'cause I don't have my records anyway."

"So? We'll go, fill out what information we can, and find out what you need to have. Then tomorrow you and Dad can go back and finish." I was pretty sure Dad would have to be with her to officially register anyway.

"Why do you even care? Why don't you just go play with your stupid car and leave me alone!"

"Dad wanted me to take you in today, and I'm not gonna give him a reason to kick me out. Besides, you're my sister," I finished lamely.

She gave me a dirty look. "Oh, yeah, that means a lot."

"Will you just go brush your teeth!" I stormed across the living room floor and snapped the TV off. "I've got to get to work!"

"Fine!" She said, standing up. "I certainly wouldn't want to do anything that would mess up anyone's schedule here! I mean, it's not like I actually expected Dad to take time off to talk to me and show me around, so I really don't expect it of you, either!" Kayla turned and ran to the bathroom, slamming the door behind her.

I sat down on the couch, really confused. I could understand her being upset about Dad not sticking around today. But when I did try to talk to her, she acted like she didn't want me around.

Sooner than I expected, she was back. Her hair was pulled back in a ponytail and she was wearing dark glasses. She had a different skirt on. It was still short, but not too bad. "Come on," she said crisply, holding her head high. "Let's get this over with."

I followed her out of the trailer. Barely glancing over her shoulder, she said, "I assume we're not taking the heap?"

"No."

She nodded and kept walking fast. I followed behind, not changing my usual comfortable stride. Her lead increased, but she stopped and waited at the entrance to the trailer park.

"Which way?" she asked when I had almost caught up.

I inclined my head to the left and she made a quick turn and set off again.

"We're not in that big of a hurry," I called after her.

Either she ignored me or she was already too far ahead to hear. She stopped at each intersection, waited until I was close enough for her to ask "Which way?" and then set off again.

"You don't have to run," I said.

"I'm not running," she called over her shoulder. "I just always walk fast."

I felt like the world's biggest fool, following her like that, but I wasn't going to run to keep up with her. For someone who had acted upset that I wasn't taking the time to talk to her, she sure could move fast.

At the third intersection, she turned around so quick she nearly fell on her face. I watched her carefully on the next block. Some of her steps were jerky, twice she tripped over small rises in the sidewalk, and once she appeared to trip over her own two feet.

When she stopped again, I didn't answer her question right away. I waited until I was almost next to her so I wouldn't have to raise my voice.

"We're going into the café over there," I said, nodding my head toward our town's only 24-hour diner.

"Wh—brrrp . . ." she covered her mouth with her hand. "Excuse me," she said, blushing. "Why?"

"Two reasons," I said, starting across the street as soon as the last car passed. It took her a couple seconds to catch up with my long stride, which only emphasized how fast she had been walking before.

We crossed the street in silence. Finally, she said, "Well?"

"What?"

"What are the two reasons?"

"So I can grab a bite to eat," I said, pulling the door open, "and so you have a chance to sober up."

She stopped halfway through the door, and probably would have tried to back out if I hadn't stepped squarely in her way.

"Find a comfortable booth," I said in a low voice. "We'll probably be a while."

She glared at me over her shoulder and I gave her a light push to get her moving.

She walked directly back to the last booth on the far wall, which was exactly where I wanted to go. Our town was small enough that me being here with a strange girl during a school day was going to get some talk started.

We slid into the booth, me facing the rest of the café, Kayla with her back to it. I pulled the laminated menus out of the pocket on the wall and slid one across to her. She made a face, shook her head, and pushed it back to me. She reached up and pulled her ponytail down, but left her glasses on.

"Oh, my head," she moaned. She put her head down on her arms on the table.

The waitress came over a few seconds later. "What can I get for you two kids?"

"Two cups of coffee, an order of scrambled eggs," I ignored Kayla's moan, "and an order of toast."

She nodded and looked like she was about to say something, but then just turned and walked away.

"So you get trashed on two cans of beer, huh? Good thing I stopped you when I did."

"It wasn't just two cans," she muttered.

"How many was it?"

"I don't remember. But it started with a green bottle of something I found in the cabinet."

"What was it?"

"How should I know? The label was half gone."

"And you drank it anyway?"

Her shoulders rose and fell slightly on the table. "I was looking for anything—"

"You need alcohol that bad?"

Again her shoulders rose and fell.

"How long have you been drinking?"

Kayla finally pushed herself up to a sitting position. Well, she leaned against the wall, but she was mostly sitting up. "Honestly?" she asked.

"Is there any other answer?"

She removed her dark glasses and rubbed her eyes tiredly. "About four hours."

I raised my eyebrows. "Honestly?"

"Is there any other answer?" she mimicked.

I looked at her closely. There were dark smudges under her bloodshot eyes. It would be easy to guess the redness was from the alcohol, but I reminded myself that her— *our*—mother had just died. She had probably spent a lot of time crying recently and most likely she wasn't sleeping real well, either. But that didn't explain her attitude in the shed. Still, I tried to give her the benefit of the doubt.

"Why'd you start today?"

Another lifeless shrug.

The waitress came by with our coffee. "Cream or sugar?"

"Yes, both please," I said.

"The rest of your order will be up soon," she said, setting the dispensers on the table and walking away.

I added a lot of cream to my coffee and began stirring. "You still haven't answered."

"Answered what?"

"Why start today?"

"Figured since I won't have much of a life living with a drunken trailer trash father, I might as well find a way to make it bearable."

"Did it?" I asked.

"Don't know. I need to give it a couple of days and see."

"Is the world spinning?"

"Yeah."

"Feel a little nauseous?"

"Yeah," her voice was a weak whisper.

"And you want to try feeling like this for a couple of days?"

"I'm sure it will get better. Otherwise, there wouldn't be as many drunks in the world."

"Well, here's a tip," I said, sipping my coffee. "Don't try mixing Jägermeister with beer first thing in the morning."

She made a face. "Jägermeister? Is that what was in the bottle?"

I nodded.

"How would you know? You said you don't drink."

"I don't now," I agreed, "but I know what Dad keeps

around the house." Then, to change the topic, "You should have some of your coffee."

"I hate coffee."

"Well, I'm paying for it so you're gonna drink it."

"Maybe you should have asked me before you ordered it then."

I raised my cup to her in a mock toast and took another sip. Kayla stared at hers for a few seconds, then began pouring enough sugar into it to raise the level. She took a sip. Making a face, she immediately dumped more into it. The coffee was up to the brim, and there was no way for her to lift the cup without spilling. She leaned forward, holding her dark hair back, and slurped some off the top.

The waitress came back with the eggs and toast. The café was a greasy joint, but you got a lot of food for your money. The eggs were piled high on a big plate, and there were four pieces of toast, all sliced and buttered. I pulled the eggs over in front of me and reached for the salt. Kayla pushed the toast toward me, wrinkling her nose.

"You should try to have at least a piece or two." When she didn't move, I added, "It will make you feel better."

"There's only one thing that's gonna make me feel better," she whispered. "Where are the bathrooms?"

I nodded my head to the door behind us and she bolted.

I had been aware of the looks we had been getting from the café's regulars, and now they all watched curiously. A few of them looked at me. I focused on my plate.

By the time she returned, I had finished my eggs and was on my second slice of toast.

"Feel better?"

She rolled her eyes at me.

"Well, you're not as green as you were," I said.

"Thanks," she said sarcastically. "You know just what to say to a girl."

"This isn't a date," I said.

She turned sideways in the booth, putting her feet up, and leaned back against the wall. "Wake me when you're ready to go," she said, putting her head back and closing her eyes.

"What was she like?"

Kayla opened one eye and looked at me. "Who?"

"Mom. What was she like?"

She shrugged. "She was Mom."

"I don't remember her."

"Everybody said I looked just like her, but I could never see it," she said, sighing. "She had just started to get some gray in her hair, but she dyed it black, so no one would know." Kayla shook her head and said, "She did that with everything."

"Dyed it black?" I asked in confusion.

"No," Kayla was irritated enough to open both eyes. "She covered everything up. She always had to make things look good, even if they weren't."

"What do you mean?"

"She wanted a big house, but she couldn't afford anything by herself. She bought a medium-sized one and her friend Brandi moved in with us. Maybe it wasn't the big house she wanted, it only had two bedrooms, but it was better than some trailer," she added.

I ignored the comment, and she continued, "Brandi and I shared a bedroom, but I slept on the trundle bed. And I always had to put the trundle bed back in the morning, in case we had visitors. Mom didn't want people to realize that we shared a room."

"I'm sure people figured it out eventually—" I began.

"Of course they figured it out!" Kayla exploded. "Just like they figured out that she put cheap liquor in expensive bottles when she served them! Just like they figured out that the nice clothes she wore were all secondhand. Everyone knew we were poor, but Mom had to try to cover it up, make it look better than it really was."

Kayla dropped her voice a little bit. "I got lice a couple of times. But each time I had to stay home, Mom had a different reason. One time I had strep throat, once I had a cold, and once she said I had chicken pox. But then I really got the chicken pox three weeks later! Mom didn't care. She just didn't want to be embarrassed."

She was looking at her hands, her long hair hiding her face. She shook her head and whispered, "She couldn't stand to be embarrassed, but she embarrassed me every chance she got."

I waited a few seconds, but Kayla stayed quiet. Finally I asked, "How did she embarrass you?"

"She was always bringing guys around, trying to find some rich man to marry her and give her the life she thought she deserved. Of course, she had to act like she was rich. So she'd bring these guys over and cook them real expensive meals, and I was their entertainment. I either didn't have enough makeup on, or I had too much on; my hair was too staticky, it was greasy, it was ugly; the shirt was too baggy, it was too tight . . . once, she told the guy that apparently it was time for me to start wearing bras! And another time, when she brought home some doctor, she asked him if it was normal for a girl to turn thirteen before getting her first period!

"I tried so hard to do things right so she couldn't find something to say about me, but she always came up with something new. Then I tried not to be around when she brought new guys home. But she insisted."

I was quiet while Kayla stirred her sugary coffee. All in all, I didn't think those things sounded so awful, but I hadn't been there.

"At least she loved you enough to spend time with you," I said finally, "even if there were other guys there."

Kayla shrugged.

I took a deep breath. "She never mentioned me?"

"No."

It was the answer I was expecting, but it still hurt.

"I'm sure that was just part of her act," Kayla said. "You know, I'm sure she thought it was better to pretend to be saddled with only one kid instead of two."

"She wasn't saddled with me for very long," I said bitterly.

Kayla played with her spoon for a couple of minutes. "So what's Dad like?"

"What you saw is what you get."

Her eyebrows rose. "Seriously?"

I laughed. "Yeah. He's almost never home, and when he is, he's drinking and watching TV."

"I've gotta get out of here," she said, almost to herself.

I stirred my coffee for a few seconds, to get control of my voice. She had said what I wished for every day. "What about Brandi? Could you go stay with her?"

"No. She only put up with me to get the cheap rent."

"Anyone else you could go to?"

For a second, I thought she was going to say something, but then she changed her mind and shook her head. "I'm stuck here. Like Dad said, no one else would take me." Her hard attitude was back; there was no self-pity in her voice.

There really wasn't anything I could say to that.

Kayla looked at me. "So Mom was a pushy wanna-be, and Dad's a lazy slob. What are you?"

I reached for my wallet. "You seem to be feeling better. It's time to get going to school."

"You're not gonna answer the question?"

I tossed a couple of bills on the table.

"Stetson?"

"Stet. Please just call me Stet."

"Stet, then. Where'd the name come from anyway?"

"You saw all of Dad's old trophies. He was a cowboy, through and through. He wanted me to be one too."

"And you're not."

I shrugged.

"You know where my name comes from?"

"Not a clue."

She laughed. "Neither do I. I asked Mom a couple of times. Once she said Kayla was a character she liked on an old soap, and another time she said she had met a really rich lady named Kayla."

"And she wanted you to be one too."

"Guess so."

"What do *you* want to be?"

"Well, sometimes I sure feel like I'm living in a soap

opera, but I'm no actress. And you know I'm not rich."

"So you haven't lived up to your name."

"Not yet."

"But you'd like to be rich." She nodded. "Do you want to be an actress?"

Kayla blushed. "A little," she admitted. "I think it'd be neat to be famous."

"Stay in this town, and you might change your mind."

"Why?"

"It's small. People always know your business, and if they don't, they're trying to find out."

"So that brings us back to the question, who and what are you?"

I slid out of the booth and stood up.

"Stet?"

"Come on, we're late enough already," I said.

She muttered something under her breath, but I couldn't hear it. We walked together the rest of the way to school, in a silence, lost in our own thoughts.

It wasn't that I didn't want to answer her question.

I just didn't know how.

CHAPTER FIVE

WE WALKED through the deserted halls to the main office. It was the middle of fourth hour, and almost everyone was in class. Two or three people were out wandering with hall passes, and one of them turned out to be Chip.

I saw him first, and I expected him to pass without saying anything, the way he always had. Instead, a big grin lit up his face.

"Stetson, my man!" He exclaimed, shaking my hand vigorously. "When you make a deal, you really come through!"

I shrugged, embarrassed. "It was no big thing."

"Dude, have you even heard what happened?"

"No. Why?"

"Pepper was so upset, she had to go home! And she's not even back today! I think you pushed her over the edge, man!"

That bothered me, but I didn't say anything. Kayla was staring with open curiosity.

"Here," he said, handing me a folded up bill, "I know we only said ten, but for getting her to quit, that deserves a bonus."

I pushed it back at him without even looking at the number on it. "She hasn't quit yet," I said, hoping I was right.

Chip shrugged. "If she hasn't yet, I'm sure you can make her do it before the semester's over."

I smiled. "I doubt I'll be in her class anymore."

"Why? Is it true? They're really expelling you?"

"What?" That shook me.

"I heard you might get expelled for it. I hope not, man." He looked down the hall. Following his glance, I saw one of the security guards heading our way. "I gotta get gone," he said, shaking my hand again. "See ya around."

He took off in the direction of the library, flashing his pass at the guard as he went by.

"Come on, Kayla."

"What was that all about?"

"Nothin'."

"You don't get expelled for *nothin'*. Come on, tell me! What'd you do?" Her eyes sparkled with excitement.

"I don't want to talk about it, all right?"

"You know I'll find out anyway."

"I said I'm not gonna talk about it!"

"All right, all right. Sheesh." She looked idly around the hall for a second, then, "Why didn't you introduce me? He was cute."

I glared at her as I pulled the door to the office open.

"Well, he was," she muttered as she walked past me.

Mrs. Beard glanced up at Kayla. "Hello. May I help—" she broke off when she saw me. Her voice dropped ten degrees. "Stetson. What are you doing here?"

"My sister needs to register for school."

Those pale blue eyes were frosty as she looked Kayla over. "I wasn't aware you had a sister."

"Neither was he," Kayla said easily.

"No need to get smart," Mrs. Beard began, looking over the rims of her glasses at us.

"Sorry," I said quickly. "She's been with my mom. We haven't spent much time together."

"Regardless, you need to have a parent with you to register."

"Can we at least get the paperwork so we can start filling it out?" I asked.

Just then the door to Mr. Johnson's office opened. Ms. Pepper started to step out, but when she saw me, she kind of fell back in. There was no sign of her trademark perma-smile.

Mr. Johnson's face froze when he saw me. Then he barked, "Stetson! Get in here!"

I had been sent to see Mr. Johnson many times, but I had never seen him this mad. His face was so red it was nearly purple, and the tendons on his neck were sticking out. He knew I hated being called Stetson, and he knew I hated being yelled at. He was furious.

I turned to Kayla, sighing. "Get the paperwork and then wait for me. I shouldn't be too long."

"That's what you think," Mrs. Beard said, loud enough for me but not for Mr. Johnson.

"Wait right there for me," I repeated, pointing to the extra chairs in the office.

"We'll see how long it takes you," Kayla said.

"Stetson!" Mr. Johnson barked again.

I put on my best relaxed face, and walked calmly into the office.

Mr. Johnson barely waited for me to get all the way inside before slamming the door shut. I jumped in spite of myself.

Ms. Pepper was sitting in one of the chairs, glaring at

me. Mr. Kincaid, one of the school counselors, was sitting next to her, watching me carefully.

"Sit down," Mr. Johnson said sternly.

Instead, I looked at Ms. Pepper and said as sincerely as I could, "I'm sorry about yesterday. It wasn't anything personal."

Ms. Pepper gave a choked-out kind of laugh and said, "Well, it certainly felt personal!"

"Sit down, Stetson!" Mr. Johnson repeated. "This is not something you can simply sweep away with an apology."

"I wasn't trying to sweep it away," I protested. "I just wanted her to know. It wasn't personal. It wasn't supposed to affect her like this."

"Ha," Ms. Pepper said mostly to herself, sniffling.

"What was it supposed to do?" Mr. Kincaid asked.

I shrugged. "Get us out of a quiz."

Ms. Pepper raised bloodshot eyes to me. "You tormented and humiliated me just to get out of a *quiz?*"

Shifting from one foot to another, I repeated, "It wasn't supposed to be that bad."

"Don't make this any worse by lying!"

"I'm not!"

"You've never cared about your grades, Stetson!" she snapped. "There's no way you'd do this over one little *quiz!*"

"I do care about my grades," I said quietly.

Ms. Pepper put her hand over her eyes, shook her head, and muttered something I couldn't hear.

"So why was it important to get out of the quiz?" Mr. Kincaid asked, watching me with the concerned look all counselors must master before they get their degree.

I shrugged.

"We've heard rumors, Stetson," Mr. Johnson said. "Rumors that this—this—insensitive prank—was the result of a bet."

I shrugged again.

Mr. Johnson threw down the pen he had been taking notes with. "You're going to have to start cooperating with us, Stetson!"

Widening my eyes, I said, "I have been. I suspended myself and I apologized as soon as I saw Ms. Pepper again. I think that's very cooperative."

"Wrong! You skipped school yesterday, and you're four class periods late today. Now you're being defiant, and before you left yesterday—I don't even know where to start on the list of violations."

"I did not skip school yesterday!" I protested, "I just suspended myself because I knew that's what you would do—"

"Stetson," Mr. Kincaid said mildly. I stopped and looked at him, sensing that he was the only one who wasn't seriously pissed at the moment. "Why don't you sit down? We're going to be here awhile."

As I did, Ms. Pepper said, "Do I have to be here for all of this? I took a sick day for a reason. I would really like to go home."

Mr. Johnson nodded. "I understand, and I'm glad you were willing to come in and talk to us about it today. What would you like to see happen as a result of this?"

Ms. Pepper cackled a half-crazy sounding laugh again. "I already told you," she said coldly. I almost asked what that was, but the grim faces on Mr. Johnson and Mr. Kincaid stopped me. "Short of that, I'd like to see to it that Stetson is never in my classroom again. *Ever.*"

Ms. Pepper was a favorite teacher because she was always so upbeat and friendly, but I had never had anyone stare at me with as much hatred as she did right then.

Refusing to let her faze me, I nodded. "I was going to suggest I be transferred to Mrs. Dobson's class."

The look on Mr. Kincaid's face almost made me laugh. Mrs. Dobson was the exact opposite of Ms. Pepper—the kids hated her. She gave a lot of notes and a lot of lectures. But I didn't care. I could follow her stupid rules. Ms. Pepper looked only slightly less shocked.

Mr. Johnson's expression never gave anything away. "I don't believe it will be that easy, Stetson," he said. He made another note and then looked up at Ms. Pepper. "Go home and rest," he said gently. "We'll take care of this."

She stood up to leave. When she reached the door, I said, "Ms. Pepper, I really am sorry."

She didn't even turn to look at me. As the door clicked shut behind her, I suddenly realized that I was in way over my head.

"Stetson, do you even know why I'm in on this conference?" Mr. Kincaid asked.

"No."

"Because what you did yesterday constituted sexual harassment. Your actions and comments were extremely degrading to Ms. Pepper as a female. It could fall into the category of verbal abuse."

I felt sick. I could only hope that it didn't show.

"Your actions yesterday include defiance, intimidation, and truancy," Mr. Johnson said from his desk. "And I'm investigating the reports of gambling as well."

"Making a bet is hardly gambling," I said.

"So you admit there was a bet?"

"I didn't say that."

"Who was the bet with?"

"I never said there was a bet."

He glared at me.

I sighed. "You said that someone else had said there was a bet involved. Now you're saying it was gambling. If there *was* a bet, it wasn't gambling, it was . . . a dare."

"So who dared you?" Mr. Kincaid asked.

I shook my head and looked at my hands.

"Stetson, covering for somebody who may have gotten you expelled is not—"

"You can't expel me over this!"

Mr. Johnson laughed.

"You can't—can you?"

Mr. Kincaid nodded.

"This incident by itself, maybe not." Mr. Johnson tapped the thick folder in the center of his desk. "Over this combined with everything else you've done in the last year, absolutely."

My stomach lurched. "But I'm going to graduate in May!"

"I don't think you are, Stetson."

They both just sat there, staring at me, satisfied that they had finally struck a nerve. They had no idea how right they were.

"Please," I said desperately. "I've got to graduate. I'll go to any class you want me to, I won't skip school again, I won't be late, whatever. Just let me graduate."

Mr. Kincaid and Mr. Johnson exchanged glances.

There was a knock on the door. Mrs. Beard opened it, just barely.

"Sorry to interrupt, but we've got a situation that needs your attention, Mr. Johnson."

He stood up quickly. "I'll be right back," he said. "See what you can work out," he added to Mr. Kincaid as the door shut behind him.

"How many fights does he break up each day?" I asked.

"You think that's a fight?"

"Yeah. It's the only thing she'll interrupt a conference for."

"You've had a lot of conferences with him."

I shrugged.

"But never for fights."

"Nope."

"Or gambling, drinking, smoking, or drugs."

I grinned. "You read my file."

Mr. Kincaid didn't smile. In fact, he got even more stern. "All you do are stupid, childish pranks. Freeing mice, eating live goldfish in the cafeteria, putting a soft porn movie in the VCR before history class, humiliating teachers—it's quite a list. The problem is that it's a long one."

Again I shrugged. "I've got to do something to pass the time."

"But you don't worry a lot about passing classes." I opened my mouth, but he continued, "Oh, yes, you pass them, but not with great grades or with any effort. According to your files, you're very bright, and you do class work, but you never do homework. And you insist that graduating is important to you." Mr. Kincaid leaned forward. "This all seems to contradict itself. Could you please explain what it is you're trying to do?"

"Graduate," I said, simply.

Mr. Kincaid shook his head and leaned back. "You're going about it in a very strange way."

I didn't answer. He could try to analyze me all he wanted, but I wasn't here for therapy. I just wanted my stupid diploma so I could get on with my life.

"Given your past record, Mr. Johnson is seriously considering beginning the expulsion process. Can you give me any reason why he shouldn't?"

"I want to graduate!"

"Have you thought about getting your GED?"

I rolled my eyes and shook my head.

"Why not?"

"Why should I?" I countered.

"Because it will give you almost as many opportunities as a diploma, but it doesn't require sitting in a classroom where you'll be tempted to cause trouble."

"So why don't you tell everyone to go get a GED and just shut down the high schools?"

Acknowledging my point, he grinned a little sadly. "A diploma will open some doors that a GED won't," he admitted. "There are a lot of places that will only accept you if you have a diploma."

"I want my diploma." I was beginning to feel like a skipping CD. "What will it take for me to be able to stay here?"

"What are you willing to do?" he countered.

"I asked first."

He raised his eyebrows.

I sighed. "Okay, okay. I guess I'll try not to be such a smart-ass."

"You'll *try*?" he said skeptically.

"Old habits are hard to break," I said, "but I'll *promise* not to disrupt classes or get suspended for the rest of this semester."

"Promises are what you're going to have to give Mr. Johnson," Mr. Kincaid agreed. "But I don't think you're giving enough to encourage him to keep you."

"No more suspensions till I graduate," I said, wincing. That would really cut into my finances.

Mr. Kincaid started to say something, but the door opened and Mr. Johnson stepped back in. "Well," he said, rubbing his hands together briskly, "what have we accomplished in here?"

"Stetson is interested in signing a success contract, in hopes that he'll be able to graduate in May."

"A success contract?" I said in confusion.

"Just writing down what we agree to today," Mr. Kincaid reassured me.

"That true?" Mr. Johnson asked me.

"Yessir," I said.

"I'm going to be very honest and say that I'm not sure it's worth our time," Mr. Johnson said. "I'm not convinced you can abide by the rules."

"I will," I said as earnestly as I could.

"If we take the time to do this right now," he said very sternly, "it will be a one-time deal. You break any of the guidelines we set up in the contract, and you're *out*, no second chances. Is that clear?"

Mr. Johnson and I locked gazes. I hated that he had already written me off. I wasn't going to give him the satisfaction of breaking me.

"He knows that this is his last chance. Don't you, Stetson?" Mr. Kincaid said.

I nodded.

"Do you want to call your father or should I?" Mr. Johnson asked, reaching for the phone.

"What for?"

"For this contract. I have to have a parent's signature on it."

"He won't come down."

"Now, Stet, I know your father's been reluctant to get involved in the past, but—"

"He'll tell you to just expel me instead."

I could feel Mr. Kincaid staring at me. Even though Mr. Johnson knew my father's track record, it still took him a couple of seconds to close his mouth.

"He'd have to come down to sign the expulsion papers, too."

I shrugged. "He won't." I nodded toward the door. "My sister's out there trying to register. She probably won't be able to because he won't take the time to come down here."

"I see," Mr. Johnson said slowly. "Then I guess we'll just have to proceed."

We spent another fifteen minutes working out the "success contract" and then we all signed it. I knew that if Mr. Kincaid hadn't been there, I would have been expelled and that would have been that. As it was, we hit one part of the contract and I flat out refused to go on.

"Stetson agrees to seek counseling regarding sexual harassment and anger management," Mr. Johnson said as he wrote.

"No."

He looked up and blinked. "Excuse me?"

"No. I'm not going to a shrink. No."

"Stetson, it's—"

"No."

"Stetson—" Mr. Kincaid began again.

"No. Look, I don't have any money. I barely have enough to eat twice a day. I'm not going to pay to go see some stupid shrink." I started shaking.

Mr. Johnson and Mr. Kincaid exchanged glances again. Knowing they wanted to say something but not in front of me was beginning to get irritating.

"I already told you it wasn't anything personal, and it certainly wasn't sexual. If it had been a Mr. Pepper, I would have done something to get to him, too. I was just trying to get my ten bucks."

"So there *was* a bet," Mr. Johnson said triumphantly.

I bit my lip.

"You're that financially strapped, huh?" Mr. Kincaid asked from the corner. "You've pulled all these stunts just to get extra money, and that money just goes for food?"

"You don't see me in any designer clothes, do you?" I asked, fingering the frayed edge of my jacket.

Mr. Kincaid studied me carefully for a moment, then said, "Instead of going to a counselor outside of school, would you agree to come in and see me once a week?"

"You don't have time for that," Mr. Johnson said to him.

"I'll make time," Mr. Kincaid said.

"I don't need your pity," I said.

"It's not pity. And you said you'd do anything to grad-uate, remember?"

"Yeah."

"So you'll come see me once a week?"

"During school?" I was already giving up too much work time.

"Yes, during regular hours."

"Okay. I can handle that."

"You could at least be grateful," Mr. Johnson said sharply. "He's making a big sacrifice just to help you out."

I glared at Mr. Johnson.

"Let's get this done," Mr. Kincaid said easily. "We've all got a lot of things to do today."

By the end of the contract, I had agreed not only to see Mr. Kincaid once a week, but not to get suspended, skip school, be tardy, or cause any kind of disruption. I would also be transferred to Mrs. Dobson's class, if she agreed.

"What if she doesn't?" I asked.

Mr. Kincaid shrugged. "Then you'll have to find another way to earn that credit," he said.

If Mr. Johnson reminded me that this was my last chance once, he must have said it at least twenty-five times. When we were done, we all signed it and shook hands.

I got up to go. "Should I come back tomorrow?"

Mr. Johnson consulted his calendar. "You were truant yesterday and late today. We'll give you a one-day suspension for that, and a two-day suspension for what you did to Ms. Pepper. Come back on Monday."

"Fresh week for a fresh start," Mr. Kincaid said.

"Okay," I said, even though I was seething. Mr. Johnson knew I hadn't been late today, and I hadn't skipped yesterday. I had given myself exactly the punishment he had chosen—two days suspension. But because he hadn't assigned it, he decided it didn't count.

Mr. Kincaid stood up. "I'd like to walk out with you, Stetson, if you don't mind."

I shrugged. He opened the office door for me. He said something to Mr. Johnson, but I was looking for Kayla and didn't hear him.

"Excuse me," I said to Mrs. Beard, "where's my sister?"

She blinked at me over her glasses. "She left about fifteen minutes ago."

I groaned.

"You might want to collect her papers."

"What?"

"I took the time to get all the forms together, she sat over there for about twenty minutes, and then she left. Without the forms." It was easy to tell that Mrs. Beard was far from pleased.

I walked over to the chairs and picked up the papers. On the top one "See ya later, Stet!" was written in big loopy letters. I ground my teeth and apologized to Mrs. Beard.

"I didn't know you had a sister," Mr. Kincaid said.

"Long story."

"Maybe we'll talk about it later."

"Maybe."

"Look, Stetson—"

"Please just call me Stet."

"Okay, Stet. I wanted to talk to you about the lunch program we have here."

"What?"

"For families with minimal income. We have federally

supported lunch programs, and I'm sure—"

"Thanks, but I don't usually eat lunch anyway."

"But Stet, you could eat for free once a day, depending on your family's income."

"No thanks," I said.

"Stet—"

"Look," I said, stopping in the hallway and making him stop too. "I appreciate that you're trying to help me, really I do. But I don't take charity from anybody, okay? Not even our lousy government. I'm doing okay on my own."

"Are you?" he asked quietly.

"Yes," I said, even though it surprised me that he asked. "I'll be back Monday. When do you want me to come check in with you?"

"During your lunch hour."

"But that—"

"You said you don't eat, right?"

I stared at him for a second, then just said, "Yeah. Okay. See you Monday." And I turned and walked out the door.

CHAPTER SIX

I WALKED into the salvage yard, ready to work hard for hours and hours and forget the world that was falling apart around me.

I had looked for Kayla all the way there, even checking at the café, but I hadn't seen her. It crossed my mind to go home and see if she was there, but I decided not to. She was showing me what a big girl she was; she could find entertainment for herself.

"Where the hell have you been? I expected you here at eight!" Jason hollered from the shed doorway.

"Sorry, Jason. I'll stay late," I called back. I kept going toward the cars, though. I didn't want to stop and talk.

I stripped off my jacket and T-shirt before getting to work. The shirt was one of the better ones I had done. On the front was a huge bear's head with a flap of red flannel dangling from his tooth. The back had a shotgun lying on the ground in front of a torn-up tent.

It was chilly without my shirt, but the sun was up and I intended to get a good sweat going. Picking up two screwdrivers and a wrench, I turned to work on the cars and almost walked right into Jason.

"Don't blow me off, man," he said. "When I ask where you were, I expect an answer."

"I had to go to school."

"I thought you were suspended."

"It's a long story."

"I got all day," he said, sitting down in the bucket chair.

Sighing, I said, "I'm not sure that's long enough."

"C'mon, Stet, give. Somethin's goin' on."

I popped the hood of the Infiniti and went around to the front, sliding the tools into my back pocket.

"I'm gonna have to cut back on my hours. Weekends and after school only."

"Why?"

"They're tryin' to expel me. I signed a paper sayin' I'd be good and not skip any more days or they'll do it."

Jason shook his head. "I told you, didn't I? You've been screwin' around too much. I'm only surprised it took 'em this long to nail your sorry butt."

"I ain't done nothin' that bad," I grunted, working on the battery bolt.

"No," he agreed, "you've just done a whole lotta nothin's."

"Yeah," I said. "That's what Johnson and Kincaid were saying."

"Who's Kincaid?" Jason knew all about Mr. Johnson.

"Our school counselor." I pulled the battery out of the car and set it down. We'd check its charge later. I moved over to the distributor cap.

"They gonna try to therapy you?"

I snorted. "I know you think they should."

"Stet, the list of things you need help with is endless."

"Yeah, but it begins with a lazy boss who only likes to work his jaw jabbering at me."

"You're gettin' mouthy for someone who shows up late."

I laughed and tossed the distributor cap next to the battery. Fan belts were next on my list.

"You gonna start seeing a social worker again?" he asked quietly.

"Nope."

"It ain't a crime to get a little help, Stet."

I put the screwdriver down. "Why does everyone think I need help all of a sudden?"

"Maybe 'cause we think you got it too hard too young and you need a break."

"Well, I don't. And I don't have it so bad. I know kids who have it worse. Dad don't beat me or nothin'."

"No," Jason said. "But he ain't never helped you neither. How long have you been on your own now?"

"I'm not on my own. I still live with Dad."

"You know what I mean." He stood up and came over to the car. "How long have you been buying your own food and clothes? How long have you been staying home alone and taking care of yourself?"

I shrugged. "Don't know."

"Can you remember a time when you weren't?"

"No."

Jason put his hand on my shoulder. "I know it pissed you off when that social worker bought you a pair of shoes back when you was in grade school. I won't pretend to understand why. But I do know that you haven't let nobody help you since then. Sometime, you're gonna have to. It's the way the world works, Stet. People help each other out."

"I don't see people helpin' you or Dad or John Stevens or Tony."

"We help each other out. You may not see it, 'cause we don't brag about getting help, but we do. It don't make you less of a man."

"I take help from you," I began.

"When? You know you could stay with me, but you won't. Hell, you won't even let me give you a lift home half the time!"

"You live the other way!"

Jason just stared at me with his good eye.

"Okay, okay, point taken. Can I get back to work now?"

"Yeah." Jason took a few steps away and then stopped. "I'll be runnin' out for lunch in a little bit. Want anythin'?"

I started to say no, the way I always did, but I stopped myself. "A burger and soda would be great."

Jason smiled slightly, nodded, and left me with the rest of the pieces to sort out.

● ● ●

Two hours later, I heard someone clearing his throat. I pulled my head out from under the dash of the Chevy, blinking in the bright light.

"Could I get a hand here?"

Jason was loaded down with two brown bags, a large bag of chips, a liter of soda, and a six-pack of beer.

I stood up and quickly relieved him of the soda and chips.

"How's the back seat?"

"Upholstery's stained, but it's comfortable enough for a picnic bench," I said. I had already pulled the front seats out, so there would be plenty of leg room too.

I climbed in on the driver's side, and Jason got in on the passenger side. We left all four doors wide open. I cracked the soda and took a few gulps.

"Ahhh," I said, holding the cold bottle to the side of my neck. "That's just what I needed."

"How'd you make out with the Infiniti?" Jason asked as he rummaged through the paper bags.

"Got one real nice condition leather seat for you. Almost all of the engine looks sellable. The oil pan was cracked, and one of the belts looks worn. Oh, and the muffler and exhaust pipes were totaled in the crash."

Jason nodded. "Good. You got it all stocked away?"

"Yep."

He tossed me a burger. I started to unwrap it, and he almost caught me in the chin with the second one when he tossed it.

"I only asked for one."

"It took me a while to get it. I figured your appetite had grown."

I started to protest, but then just muttered, "Thanks."

We chewed in silence for a few minutes.

"How's this bucket of rust looking?"

"Like a bucket of rust," I said. "The battery's rusted in, the mirrors are rusted over, the hub caps are rusted through—"

"Okay, okay. Don't waste a lot of time on it, then. Save yourself for the profits."

"I will," I said. "But they installed a sweet sound system that's definitely worth working on."

"Good enough."

Again we were quiet. It wasn't an easy quiet, though.

"What's up?" I finally asked.

"What do you mean?"

"Somethin's goin' on, and you're not talkin' about it."

"It ain't nothin'," he said. Then, "Who were you trailin' this mornin'?"

I looked at him in surprise. "You saw me?"

"And her," he nodded. "She looked fit to spit at you. You dumpin' her or somethin'?"

I laughed. "Not even close. But now I know why you were so pissed this mornin'. You thought I skipped on you for a girl."

He grinned. "Well, you are young and stupid and full of lust."

"It ain't nothin' like that."

"So what's it like?"

I put the last of the burger in my mouth and washed it down with soda, but I couldn't taste a thing.

"Her name's Kayla. Turns out she's my sister."

Jason's eyebrows went up and he whistled low, but he didn't ask any questions. He didn't need to. Within minutes, I had laid out all of the previous evening's events, and the morning's as well.

"You haven't gone home to check on her?"

"Nope."

In one swift motion, he took off his old baseball cap and whacked me upside the head with it. "What the hell are you thinking?"

Wincing and rubbing my head, I responded, "I'm thinking she bailed on me and she wants to prove she can do what she wants. I'm thinking I didn't know she even existed until last night and I don't owe her a damn thing. I'm thinking that she's a spoiled little snot that needs to get over herself, and maybe taking a few bumps is how she'll do it!" By the time I finished, I was nearly yelling.

"What are you so pissed about?" Jason yelled back.

"She—" I pushed myself out of the car.

"She what?"

I didn't answer, just stared off at the rest of the junk-yard.

"She what?" Jason had gotten out of the car too.

"Nothin'."

"I know you, Stet. I've known you longer and better than most people. But I've never seen you mad like this."

I shook my head. "It's nothin'."

"You're lyin'."

I shook my head again.

"You're lying to me," Jason said quietly.

I spun around. "Back off," I said, matching his tone.

We stared at each other for a few moments, then finally he held up his hands.

"Okay. I give. I'll back off."

I gave a short nod.

"I guess I should let you get back to work."

"Thanks."

"Try to get to the original Beetle next," he said, walking away. "Their parts are in bigger demand these days."

"Yessir," I said saluting him.

He never turned around, but he flipped me off just the same.

● ● ●

The cars were cold and hard, but they were also the best things in my life. I understood them. They never did anything to hurt me, and they always listened to my confessions without judgment. And although all cars are predictable, each one was unique enough to keep me from getting bored.

I lost myself in the cars, the way I always do, and the next time I became aware of the world, it was nearly dark and I had to pee.

I quickly put the tools in the box, then stashed it in the half-stripped new Beetle. Not only had I finished stripping the classic Beetle and Chevy, but I had also stocked all their parts. I had worked like a man possessed.

As I walked toward the salvage office, I wondered why Jason hadn't come to get me at five, the way he always did. Even when I told him I was going to work late, he checked around five to make sure I didn't want to go home.

I ducked around to the bathroom before going into the office. When I came in the front door, everything was still. The thought crossed my mind that maybe Jason had already left, but I rejected it almost immediately. He wouldn't leave without saying good-bye. He couldn't be that mad.

"Jason?"

"Yeah." His voice was low, weak, and almost directly beside me. I jumped.

He was sitting down behind the register to the left of the door. I don't think I had ever seen him do that before, unless he was on the phone, and then it was only for a few minutes at a time. It looked like he had been there forever.

"You okay?"

"Yeah." His voice was still low, and his face was kind of gray.

"I don't believe you."

He waved his hand. "I just got some kind of bug. Couldn't keep lunch down."

"So why didn't you go home?"

"Got work to do."

I raised my eyebrows. "Don't look like you're doin' much now."

He snorted. "Sure I am. Supervisin' a disrespectful teenage employee. Toughest job there is."

"Whatever."

His eyes closed for a long moment.

"Jason?"

"Yeah." He opened his eye. A little.

"What's goin' on?" I was starting to get a little spooked. I didn't know CPR, and I was afraid he might need it soon.

He shook himself a little. "Nothin'. Just got some bug is all. You're probably right, though. I ought to get on home." He looked at me sternly. "You ought to get on home, too."

I saluted him. "Yessir, that's just what I was gonna do."

He flipped me off, but his hand didn't have much snap to it.

"Go on, get out of here," I said. "I'll lock up."

"You'll go home," he said, and I couldn't tell if it was a question or an order.

"I already said that," I said. "You gettin' senile or somethin'?"

"Smart-ass," he muttered, and pushed himself out of the chair. As he stood up, he went from gray to white and kind of swayed on his feet.

I took a half step forward, ready to catch him if he fell, but he opened his eye wide and grabbed hold of the counter.

"Man, you don't look so good," I fretted.

"Man, I don't feel so good," he said. "That's why I'm goin' home."

"You sure you can make it?" I asked worriedly. "You want me to drive you home?"

"What, and live with the guilt that you had to walk an extra ten miles home? No thanks."

"You could just pay me for the time it takes me to walk home," I said. I was joking, but I was still watching him carefully. He looked like he could fall over at any minute.

"Can't afford that. Nope, I'll just drive myself straight home. You won't mind if I don't offer you a ride tonight?"

"Now who's being the smart-ass?"

He laughed weakly, and leaned against the door frame for a moment. "Make sure you lock up."

"I will."

"You'll be here tomorrow?"

"The rest of the week."

He nodded. "Good. I don't know if I'll be in or not."

"Don't worry about it. I've got it covered."

"Thanks, Stet," he said as he shuffled to his car. "You may be an occasional screwup, but you're a good kid."

"Thanks," I said, even though I wasn't convinced it was a compliment.

I stood in the door and watched until he was out the gate. He actually turned on his blinker, which meant he was driving very carefully. Then I went to the back of the office to get my other two wheels.

As I picked them up for the walk home, I hoped Jason would be better by next week. I wouldn't be able to come in and work days anymore. I had to graduate.

CHAPTER SEVEN

ALL THE way home I argued with myself. I wanted to get the wheels on the car and work on some paint designs. I knew what colors I wanted, but I hadn't figured out the right design yet. But part of me knew that I should try to talk to Kayla some more and at least find out what she had done all day.

As it turned out, the trailer was dark when I got there, so I just went around back to the shed. I stopped short when I saw the door hanging open. Then I dropped both wheels and charged in.

All four of the bare bulbs were on, casting stark shadows. The car stereo was on, sending vibrations through the air with every bass downbeat. Both doors were wide open, and two feet were hanging out the passenger side.

"What the hell are you doing?" I yelled.

Kayla sat up fast, swayed, and then covered her mouth with both hands. I grabbed her arm and yanked, barely getting her out of the car before she threw up. I left her sprawled on the dirt floor, and shook my arm and foot in disgust. Some of it had landed on me.

She looked up at me, bleary-eyed, and said, "Hey, Stetson, whazzup?" Then she put her hands on her head and said, "Oh, I feel like crap."

"Good!" I retorted as I reached in and turned the stereo off. "What the hell are you doing in here?"

"Just hangin' out. You're right. These seats *are* comfortable."

"How did you get in here? I know you saw me lock it this morning." I could feel the only key still in my pocket. I never went anywhere without it.

Wincing, she whispered, "Not so loud, 'kay?"

Cursing, I went to the door. The padlock was still locked and in one piece, holding both parts of the latch shut. She had simply removed the screws on the latch and taken the whole thing off.

"Damnit, Kayla, don't you know that people lock things when they want you to stay out?"

She didn't answer, and I turned around to look at her. She had passed out in the puddle of puke.

I was sorely tempted to just leave her there. But I wanted to put the wheels on tonight, and she was in the way.

I kicked her gently in the leg. "Kayla, get up." I kicked her again, this time maybe not so gently. "Get up!" Her eyelids fluttered.

Grimacing, I bent down and picked her up, holding my breath as long as I could. I hate the smell of puke.

I half-dragged, half-carried her to the trailer, cursing the whole way, and then leaned her against the side while I opened the door. I got her back to my bedroom and almost laid her on the bed before I thought better of it. I left her on the floor, on her side in case she puked again. I even moved the trash can over next to her, but I doubted she would see it in time.

As I came back through the kitchen, I stopped in disbelief. On the kitchen counter was a wall of beer cans. It was four cans across and three cans up. No wonder she had puked. Briefly I thought about alcohol poisoning, but then I just pulled the front door shut. I had done what I could. I'd check on her later. If I had to, I'd go to MacGregor's and tell Dad to take her to the hospital.

Back out in the shed, I dumped two buckets of dirt over the mess she had left. Then I grabbed a screwdriver and fixed the latch. I left the door wide open to try to air out the shed.

For the next two hours I worked on the wheels, and then I rebalanced the stereo system. Once I had it back to where I wanted it, I just sat in the driver's seat, relaxing.

My car was almost finished. After saving a dollar here, fifty cents there for over a year, I had been able to order the parts that hadn't come in through the salvage yard. Jason kept telling me that I was trying too hard to make it perfect, but he just didn't understand.

The steering wheel was a sharp blue suede from a Prelude, and I had the matching plush bucket seats. The back seat was also a nice plush blue, but it was a little lighter. Not much, but I noticed it. I had gotten the blue carpet six months ago, and had used it for the floor and the four floor mats.

The engine was completely done, and the interior was only missing a dashboard, seat belt, and side panels. It still had the original dashboard, which was an ugly brown, cracked and peeling in places. I had been hoping to find an original blue board in good condition, but now I was considering one of Jason's suggestions: covering the board I had with the remaining blue carpet.

It may only be a little Honda Civic, I thought to myself, *but it looks good. It's gonna be a classy little car, sharp, not tacky.* That's why the paint job had me so concerned. It had to be just right.

I rested my head against the steering wheel, trying to clear my mind.

What I needed now was a pattern or a design or something to make it special. Flames along the front and sides could be neat, but they'd been done too many times.

Usually, when I looked at a blank piece of paper or T-shirt, I always saw an image superimposed on it. Sometimes it almost seemed as if the image was there already and my mind just pulled it out. But when I looked at my car, I was unable to see any image.

Sighing, I leaned my head back, and realized someone was standing in the door. The bare bulbs cast dark shadows in the doorway, making it impossible to tell who it was.

"Hello?" I asked, climbing out of the car.

"Hi, Stet."

"Vicky!" I grinned, trying to cover my shock. "How're you doin'?"

"I'm doin' okay," she said, bobbing her head a little. She came around the car and gave me a hug. "Haven't seen you for a while."

"Been pretty busy," I said, looking at her. She was tired, and seemed uptight about something. I wondered how long before she'd tell me what was wrong.

She looked at the car. "It's coming together nice, just like you always said it would."

I laughed. "Yeah, but it's takin' forever!"

Vicky shrugged. "They always say the good things are worth waitin' for. The engine done?"

"Yep."

"I remember all the trouble the carburetor was giving you," she said, smiling sadly.

"Yeah, but I got it back in line. She purrs for me now."

"That's good."

"How's the baby?"

"Cassie's good. Growin' fast. You ought to come see her."

"Where is she right now?"

"I left her with Mom. Tony was supposed to come home after work, but he hasn't showed yet."

"Did ya check MacGregor's?"

"Of course," she said, rolling her eyes. "But he's not there. I was hoping maybe he came by here again."

"What do you mean? Tony hasn't been over here since—since before your wedding," I said.

She nodded like that was what she expected to hear, but I was alarmed to see the tears fill her eyes. She wiped them away, but they were replaced almost immediately.

"Hey, oh, hey, don't do that," I said.

"I'm sorry, Stet," she said as she accepted my hug and leaned against my shoulder. "I know you hate to see girls cry."

"I hate to see you cry, not just any girl," I corrected.

She laughed a little, then sniffled.

"What's wrong, Vick?"

"It's hard bein' a mom, and it's hard bein' married," she said.

"I bet."

"And it's even harder when somebody starts cheatin' before the first anniversary."

"You think—" I didn't finish, but she nodded anyway. "Nah, Tony wouldn't do that to you."

She shrugged and sniffled again. "I'm almost positive he already has."

"Oh, Vick . . ." I didn't know what to say.

"There's been a couple times I've looked for him at MacGregor's when he didn't come home. He wasn't there, and when he finally did come home, he said he had been here helping with the car."

"I wish . . ." I began, feeling helpless. I felt like I had betrayed Tony by blowing his cover, and at the same time I felt like I was betraying her by not knowing where he was.

She shook her head. "I'm glad I know he's not here. Tonight when he does come home, maybe I'll get the truth out of him."

"You'll let me know if I can help?"

She nodded. I knew she wouldn't, though. Vicky and I had been very close friends, both before and after we had dated, but Tony and I had been friends first. There are some lines you just don't cross.

"How's school?"

"It's school," I said.

"I never thought I'd miss it," she said quietly. "You gonna graduate?"

"I'm trying to."

"I hope you do," she said honestly. "That'd be cool."

Smiling, I said, "You're the first person to think that."

"That's because everyone else around here is an idiot." She sighed and looked around one last time. "Well, I suppose I ought to get goin'. Mom gets tired of bein' the standby baby-sitter."

"Tell her I said hi."

"You were always her favorite."

"I wasn't around enough for her to get to know."

"That's probably why," she said, laughing.

She reached up and gave me another big hug. We held on to each other, probably a little longer than we should have. I looked up over her shoulder as we stepped apart and saw Kayla standing just inside the door.

"Well, look who's up," I drawled.

She sneered at me. "Are you gonna introduce me?"

"Kayla, this is my friend Vicky. Vicky, this is Kayla."

They both nodded, but I sensed the tension in the shed. I couldn't understand why it was there. One was my sister, the other was married to my friend, but they both seemed to be eyeing each other as a possible rival.

"Thanks, Stet," Vicky said.

"No problem."

Vicky stopped in front of the door and for a moment I didn't think Kayla was going to get out of her way. She finally did, and then glared at her back.

When Vicky was out of earshot, she spun to me. "Is that your little girlfriend?"

"Go back to bed," I said. "You're too pissed to be awake."

"I wasn't in *bed*," she snapped. "Some jerk just left me on the *floor*."

"It's my bed, and I didn't want you puking in it. Next time I'll just leave you in the dirt with your face in the puddle of puke."

I could see her trying to come up with something to say, but all that came out was a sheepish "Oh."

I went to my worktable, pulled out my notebook, and began flipping through the sketches. What I needed was the right idea. I could draw or paint anything once I had the idea.

"Where were you? I kept waiting for you to come home."

"Well, if you had waited at school like I asked, you wouldn't have had that problem."

"You took too long."

"It wasn't that long. And I was only there in the first place because of you."

"I didn't get you in trouble!"

"No, you just made me go to school when I'd been suspended."

She was quiet for a few minutes, and I thought she'd decide to leave.

"So where were you?"

"At work. Where were you?"

"I ran into that guy again—Chip? He took me out to lunch, and then I came back here and waited."

I didn't say anything.

"There's nothing in the fridge," she said. "When does Dad go grocery shopping?"

"He won't. I'll try to pick up a few things tomorrow."

"I could go."

I turned to look at her. "You're supposed to go to school tomorrow."

She shrugged. "It can wait. It'd be better to start on a Monday anyway."

"But if you start tomorrow, maybe you'll know Chip well enough to go out this weekend," I said. "Oh, but you might want to ask his girlfriend if that's okay."

"He has a girlfriend?"

"Yep."

"He didn't tell me that!" she wailed.

I looked at her in surprise. "You just went for lunch, right?"

She looked at her feet and began shuffling them in the dirt. "He didn't tell me!"

"You knew the guy for a half hour and you—"

"No! We didn't do that! But we did fool around. . . ." Her voice trailed off.

I laughed and shook my head. My sister was off to a great start.

She groaned and sat down in the doorway, holding her head in her hands.

I glanced over my shoulder. "How're you feeling?"

"Like I puked my guts out."

"Almost."

She groaned again.

"By the way, you might want to start figuring out how you're gonna replace Dad's beer."

"What do you mean?"

"I mean, that's all he keeps in the fridge. You've drunk more than two six-packs since you got here. He's gonna notice."

"I don't suppose you could . . ."

"Nope."

She was quiet for a minute, then she said, "Well, I guess he'll just have to deal with it, then."

I raised my eyebrows, but didn't say anything. She had seen Dad "deal with" things last night. It wasn't going to get any better.

"You know, your car's actually kind of cool."

"Gee, thanks," I said sarcastically. "*Kind of cool*

is exactly the look I was aiming for."

"No, I mean it. I'm sorry I called it a heap this morning."

I looked up at her. "And I'm sorry you felt the need to break in here this afternoon."

She blushed. "The trailer was boring."

"Oh, and it's a world of excitement out here."

"Seems to be for you."

I shrugged. "I like working out here."

"Have you really been workin' on it for years?"

"Almost two," I confessed.

"Well, it looks good."

"Thanks."

"How are you gonna paint it?"

I grimaced. "That's what I'm tryin' to figure out." Kayla yawned. "Why don't you go back to bed? It's late."

"It's not that late."

"Do you know what time it is?"

"No," she admitted.

"I bet it's almost midnight."

"That's not late," she protested.

"Come on," I said, closing the notebook and tossing it back on the table. "Let's go." I walked over to her, but she made no effort to get to her feet. She was staring at the tire, a lost look in her eyes. I nudged her foot.

Finally she looked up. "Why am I here?"

"Because Mom died."

"Do you think he cares?"

"I don't know." I suppose I could have given her a more reassuring answer, but I didn't like to lie. As she started to look down, I added, "But I do."

She smiled. "Thanks." We were quiet for a few seconds.

Then she said, "He came to get me right away, so I kind of thought that I meant something to him. But then, on the drive here, all he did was complain about Mom and the way I dressed and how I looked and how much trouble it was for him to take one lousy day off . . ." She shook her head. "I almost asked him why he didn't just leave me there."

"Why didn't you?"

"Brandi's not my—our—aunt or anything. She was Mom's best friend. And Dad was right last night when he said she didn't want me. She's getting married in a month and I'd just be in the way."

"What about your—our—grandmother?"

"She's in a nursing home. She can't take care of herself, much less me."

"And you're sure we don't have any other family we could go to?"

"We?"

I blushed. "You. I meant you."

"Are you sure?"

"Yeah. Dad's not my idea of Father of the Year or anything, but we know how to stay out of each other's way. Besides, I'll be graduating soon."

Kayla nodded. "I sent a letter to one of Mom's second cousins, but I don't know. I've only met her once, and she lives way out in Kansas." Again we were quiet. I was just about ready to suggest we go inside when she blurted out, "Why did she leave you here? With him?"

I clamped my mouth shut hard.

I had been thinking about that almost all day, even though I kept trying not to. Every answer I came up with was painful. I didn't want to think about the question, and the answer had been buried with the mother I could hardly remember.

Kayla moaned. "Why did she leave me nowhere to go but here with him?"

Just barely I stopped myself from pointing out the fact that at least she had gotten through her first fourteen years without him.

"He's not all that bad."

"Sure seems like it."

"He'll stay out of your way, if you'll stay out of his. He won't beat you or try to embarrass you or anything."

Kayla dashed a tear off her cheek and gave me a trembling smile. "I guess that's something."

I reached my hand down. "Come on," I said. "Time to go in."

She reached up for my hand and I pulled her to her feet. "I wish Mom had told me about you before," she said.

"Me too."

"She would have liked you."

Somehow, that was nice and painful to hear at the same time.

We stepped out of the shed and I shut and locked the door behind us. She began giggling.

"What?"

"Nothing. I just think it's funny you lock it up."

"I don't think it's funny that you broke in."

"I didn't break in—" she began. I raised my eyebrows. "I won't do it again," she finished.

"Thank you."

We walked the few steps to the trailer quickly. The living room light was on.

"Did you throw out the beer cans?" I asked quietly.

She shook her head as she opened the door.

Dad was sitting at the far end of the couch. He glared at both of us and sat up a little as we came in. You could almost feel his anger. "So who's the funny one?"

Kayla looked at me, confused.

"Who's the smart-ass who thinks they can build a shiny castle with *my* beer cans?"

Kayla opened her mouth to speak, but all that came out was a little squeak.

"I'm the architect," I said easily. I glanced over at the wall of cans. "Not my best work, but I wasn't thinkin' clearly."

"You weren't thinkin' at all if you think you can free-load off my beer."

"I'll pay for them."

"Damn right you will." He leaned back on the couch. "Glad you were smart enough to leave me a six-pack for tonight."

"Wouldn't want to leave you dry."

"Thought you didn't drink. Didn't want to kill your precious brain cells."

Kayla began moving slowly down the hall.

I shrugged.

Dad held his hand out to me. "Ten bucks."

I opened my mouth to object, but then I saw how many cans were in the wall. "I'll catch you tomorrow."

"I got to buy it tomorrow, idiot. Give me the cash now."

"I don't have it."

"Don't lie to me, boy! I know you got to stash money somewhere! You and your stupid hope that you may actually get into some school, you save pennies like a squirrel saves nuts."

"I don't have cash on me," I repeated.

He sprang up. I was surprised his beer gut let him move that fast. "I'll come beat it out of you if I have to."

"I don't have it, Dad," I was tense all over. I thought I could take him, but it would probably be a close thing. We were the same height, but he outweighed me by at least sixty pounds.

"Here," Kayla said from behind the couch.

Dad turned to her in surprise. He had forgotten she was even there, but that didn't slow him down as he ripped the ten from her hand. Then he smirked at both of us. "How cute. Baby sister sticking up for her loser big brother."

Kayla looked like she might say something, and I shook my head. I knew from past experience it wasn't worth it.

"You go to school today?"

"Yes." Kayla almost sounded meek.

I could tell she wasn't going to say anything else, so I said, "She means we picked up papers. But she can't start classes till you go in with her."

Dad swore. "I ain't got the time for that. As it is I'm gonna be short hours this paycheck, and the boss is always lookin' for an excuse to ride me." He glanced at me. "Maybe it's time you start payin' rent around here."

"Only if you start buyin' groceries," I countered quietly.

Dad glared at me.

I nodded toward Kayla. "And we'll be feedin' three now."

He turned back to Kayla. "I'll take you in on Monday. Can't lose two days' pay out of the same check."

She nodded. "Fine."

"You stay with Stetson till then. I don't need you runnin' round gettin' in trouble. He'll keep you clear."

"I don't need no baby-sitter."

Dad raised his eyebrows. "You don't want to get smart with me, girl."

Kayla tried to meet his stare, but her alcoholic courage was gone. Instead, she turned, went to my room, and slammed the door behind her.

Dad chuckled. "Glad to see one of my kids has got some sense."

CHAPTER EIGHT

THAT NIGHT I really did sleep on the couch. And when I woke up, stiff and sore, I decided I would be better off sleeping in the shed after all. At least until it started getting really cold at night. I didn't know what I'd do then.

I sat up slowly, blinking in the light. Kayla was sitting across the floor from me, leaning against the wall under the open window. That was what had woken me up. The light from the window.

"Why'd you open the blinds?" I asked, trying to see her through slitted eyes.

"It's too dark and dingy otherwise."

"I kind of like it dark. Helps me sleep."

"You sleep pretty sound," she said.

"Usually," I said, turning my neck this way and that. "But how do you know?"

"I made a lot of noise opening the blinds."

"So you were *trying* to wake me."

Kayla shrugged and tried unsuccessfully to hide her grin. "What are we doing today?"

"I've got to go to work."

"You're gonna leave me here all by myself?" she asked in a squeaky little-girl voice.

"I'm sure you'll do just fine."

"What about Dad?"

"What about him?"

"Won't he get mad? He said you were supposed to

keep me out of trouble or something."

I shrugged. "Dad probably won't remember anything about it." When she didn't look like that was enough, I added, "And if you keep yourself out of trouble, he'll never know." That still didn't seem to please her. "What's wrong?"

"I'm just not excited about spending the whole day here alone again."

"You could come to work with me—"

"Okay!"

"But it'll be boring," I finished.

"I'm sure I'll find something to keep me busy," she said quickly. "Where do you work, anyway?"

"At the salvage yard."

"The what?"

"Salvage yard. It's kind of an upscale town dump."

"I thought this was the town dump."

I grinned and shook my head. "This mansion? The butler will be most upset to hear you say that."

She smiled back at me. "How can a town dump be upscale?"

"We don't just shove stuff in a landfill. We take big appliances and cars and resell them or piece them out."

"Piece them out?"

"Take them apart and sell off the individual pieces."

"Oh." Kayla still had a blank look on her face. "So what do you do there?"

"Take stuff apart."

"Oh," she said again. "Well, I'm sure it'll be better than hanging out here."

"I wouldn't count on it," I muttered, as I swung my legs off the couch. I stood up and stretched, grimacing. I now knew where every lump in those old cushions was.

"Do you always sleep in your clothes?"

"Only when we have female company."

"I'm not really company. I'm here for a while."

"Sometimes company sticks around. Besides, you're still female."

"I didn't mean to kick you out of your room."

I shrugged again. "I won't be sleeping out here much longer. Hopefully only for eight months. You just have to leave me some drawer and closet space."

Kayla nodded, looking down at her hands.

"Come on, what's wrong?"

She shook her head, then said, "Absolutely everything."

I couldn't see her face, but I guessed she was crying, and it was pretty obvious why. To tell the truth, I was surprised she hadn't been crying more often. But I still didn't know what to say. I couldn't help her.

"Things will work out," I said.

She nodded and then sniffed twice.

"I'm gonna go shower. Then we can leave."

Again she nodded, and I left her there.

When I came back to the living room, she was gone. I wasn't surprised. And although I'd never admit it, I was a little hurt, too.

● ● ●

Jason wasn't at the yard when I got there, and I couldn't decide if I was relieved or upset. Part of me was glad he was willing to take the day off and get better. The rest of me was worried. He had to be really sick to stay home. I could count the number of times he'd done that on one hand.

I unlocked the gate and shut it behind me, but I didn't padlock the chain shut. If I had the keys to the register and shed, I would have left the gate open, even though not many people came to the yard during the week. I just didn't want to deal with the hassle of someone wanting to buy stuff and me not being able to sell it. I was pretty sure that if the gate was shut no one would try to come in.

I set to work on the new Beetle right away, and lost myself in the work. I loved taking the pieces of a car apart almost as much as I loved putting them together. When you took them apart, it reminded you how basic everything really is. Even a two-ton truck can be reduced to bolts, screws, wires, fluids, and scrap metal in a matter of hours.

As I took the cars apart, I could also get a feel for how people had treated the vehicle. Sometimes the fancy luxury cars had oil so thick I wasn't sure it had ever been changed. And the rust on the battery terminals made it look like the car had been sitting outside for years. But some of the older ones had been pampered. It was obvious from the clean oil to the full wiper fluid that they had been cared for, that the only thing that brought them to us was the blink of an eye and a final accident.

The cars could be pretty freaky, if you thought too much about the accidents. Although some of our cars have been repossessed for one reason or another and the credit company just sold them to us, and some were evidence confiscated by police, and a few were brought in by the owners, most came straight from the accident site. And a lot of times, the blood was still there.

I thought the worst I'd seen was the bloody dashboards under starred windshields. But then they brought in an old station wagon. The upholstery was bloody in the front and the back, and so was the child's car seat. I was relieved when Jason decided that car was so mangled it wasn't worth trying to piece out.

"Stetson!"

I pulled myself out from under the hood of the car and looked around.

"Stetson!"

I thought I recognized the voice, but I wasn't completely sure. Wiping my hands on my rag, I followed the voice to the yard gate. As I rounded the last row of bumpers, I could see him.

"Stetson!" Tony hollered again. He had his hands on the wire fence and was staring toward the shed.

"Over here!" I called.

He turned to me and grinned, waving his hand over his head.

I almost told him to just open the gate; after all, the chain wasn't locked. But something stopped me. He left the gate and came my way on the other side of the fence.

"Your dad said you'd be here," he said as we got closer. "I was startin' to think he was wrong."

"What's up?" I asked. My heart started thudding in my chest. It was the middle of the day, and Dad had told him where to find me. Mill accidents happen all the time. What if—

"You talk to Vicky the other day?"

It took me a second to answer, because I had expected

to hear something else. "Yeah."

"What'd you tell her?"

"Nothin'."

"You must've said somethin'. She's all worked up."

"Honest. She asked where you were, and I told her what I knew, which was nothing'."

"She's callin' me a liar since you said we ain't seen each other for months."

"We haven't."

"You're the liar! Man, we just saw each other two days ago!"

"What?"

"At MacGregor's? In the parking lot?"

"Oh," I said, blinking. "That. Well, yeah, but—"

"So now Vicky's all upset, thinkin' I'm cheatin' on her, and it's all 'cause you can't remember things. Man, I thought you was the smart one. Maybe it's time you admit you're as dumb as the rest of us and quit school."

"Tony, Vicky asked me about the last time you were over workin' on the car with me, not the last time I seen you. That's what I was talkin' about."

"You shoulda just told her you saw me a couple days ago. That woulda solved everythin'."

"You didn't tell me I was supposed to lie for you."

"I didn't ask you to lie for me—"

"That's right, you didn't tell me what was goin' on!" I interrupted. "It ain't my fault Vicky got suspicious and asked me some questions."

Tony rolled his eyes. "I thought you'd always back me, man."

"You got to let me know before I can back you!"

Looking down at the ground, Tony mumbled something I couldn't hear.

"You cheatin' on her?" I asked quietly.

"That ain't somethin' you ask about."

"It is when I'm bein' used as cover."

"Look, I got to get back to work." He started to turn away.

"Tony!" He stopped. "Are you?"

His shoulders kind of slumped before he turned back to face me. "You don't understand—" he began.

"No," I said, feeling myself begin to shake all over, "I don't. She gave up school and maybe even a scholarship for you. She's raisin' your little girl. She's done nothin' but love you."

"Stet, it's tough—" he tried again.

"Everything's tough! You deal with it. You don't cheat on your wife. That don't fix nothin'."

"You still love her, don't ya?"

"That has nothin' to do with this."

"I think it does," he said slowly. "She never understood why you broke up with her. Neither did I. But hell, when she came to me, I sure wasn't gonna worry about it. Maybe that's where I messed up."

"You're cheatin' on her."

"Sometimes," he said, shrugging.

It wasn't so much that he admitted to it that pissed me off; it was the way it didn't seem to matter to him. "You bastard."

Tony shrugged again. "Maybe you'll get a second chance with her in a couple years, when I'm done with her."

It was a good thing I hadn't told him to unlock the gate and come in. I would have torn him to pieces.

He turned and walked away from the fence, and I knew that our friendship was completely over. Now, even if he saw me passing MacGregor's, he wouldn't stop to talk or even wave.

In a way, it depressed me. But it also made me feel free.

● ● ●

"You're a—"

I didn't hear the rest. I jumped so bad I slammed my head into the hood of the car, and all I could hear was a ringing in my ears.

I put my hand up to my head, and felt a warm wetness where I part my hair. Slowly, so I didn't make the dizziness worse, I leaned around the hood.

Kayla was standing a few feet away from the car, looking out of place in her denim miniskirt and baby-pink T-shirt. Well, she would have looked out of place if she had a nicer expression on her face. The I-hate-this-so-much-I-could-chew-nails expression on her face fit in just fine.

"Oh my God, you're bleeding!" she exclaimed, her face softening and showing genuine concern.

I half grinned at her but didn't move or anything.

"Stet? You okay?"

Still grinning, I shook my head.

"What's wrong?"

"I can't decide who I should kill first. You or me."

She frowned, putting her hands on her hips. "I'm serious!"

"So am I," I said, taking a couple of slow steps forward.

She took a couple of quick steps back. "What are you doing?"

"Going over to the front shed," I said, matching my action to my words.

"It's locked," she said, falling into step with me.

I glanced at her and raised my eyebrows. "Can't you pick the lock?"

"You're really not funny," she said. "Do you have a key?"

"No, but we won't need one. The spigot on the other side isn't locked."

"You're gonna need more than just a spigot. You're bleeding pretty bad."

"I doubt it's that bad. Head wounds just bleed a lot."

"You've done this a lot?"

"Only when people sneak into a closed area and scare the crap out of me." At least she looked guilty. "Did you at least close the gate behind you?"

"No," she said slowly.

"Well, go shut it now," I said crossly, "before other people start to wander in."

She trotted off toward the gate and I went behind the shed to the spigot. I turned the water on, and then very carefully stretched out the neck of my T-shirt as far as I could. I quickly pulled it off, and immediately checked for blood. Luckily, it was fine. It wasn't my best work, but it was a design Vicky had suggested when we were dating.

The shirt itself was blue, and I had covered the back with white clouds. The front had a castle of clouds, and a dark green Corvette was racing up to it. Some guys might think it was cheesy, but it was one of my favorites.

I stuck my head under the cold running water. It didn't feel great, but I knew it had to be done. The running water would get out any rust or metal that might have gotten in the cut, and the cold would slow down the bleeding.

I lifted my dripping head. Kayla was sitting on an over-turned oil barrel, watching me.

"You've got blood on your face," she said matter-of-factly.

I splashed some water on my cheeks and scrubbed them. Then I felt through my hair for the cut, found it, and applied pressure with my palm for a few seconds. When I took my hand away, it had some blood on it, but not too much. Kayla got off her barrel and came over.

"It looks bad," she said.

"How big is it?" I asked.

She looked carefully, then said, "About the size of my pinky nail."

I looked at her manicured hands. Her pinky nail was almost an inch long. "The whole nail?"

"Well, it's about the length of the nail, but it's not nearly as wide. It's more like a scratch, really."

"Is it very deep?"

"I can't tell."

"Then I'll be fine."

"Maybe we should have someone else look at it, you know, like—" she stopped, suddenly aware that there wasn't anyone else for us to go to.

"I'm fine," I said, scooping up my shirt. I wasn't going to put it back on until I knew I was done bleeding.

For a second I thought she was going to argue with me, but she just followed me back through the maze of the yard to the cars I was working on.

I picked up the lug wrench and tried to go back to work.

Kayla came over and leaned into the hood with me. "How much more you got to do today?"

"As much as I can."

She gave an exasperated sigh. "How much longer are you gonna be working this afternoon?"

I shrugged. "I've got four more cars to do."

"How many have you done so far?"

"Today?"

"Yes."

"I've almost finished this one."

"And you've got four more to do?" she squawked.

"Yep."

"Today?"

"Well, whenever I get to them."

She slapped my shoulder. "So when can you leave?"

I put the wrench down and looked at her. "You're already bored? It's not like you've been waiting here with me all day or anything."

"I'm not bored," she said.

"Well, then, get out of my way," I said, picking up the wrench again. "I've got work to do."

"I'm hungry," she said in a small voice.

"What?"

"I'm hungry," she repeated, looking up at me with big sad eyes. "There's nothing to eat in the house and I gave the only money I had to Dad."

I groaned.

"Have you eaten lunch?" she asked. "Maybe we could go to the café, like we did yesterday."

Shaking my head, I put the wrench down again and pulled my wallet out of my pocket. I thumbed through the bills quickly, counting and trying to guess how much I'd need for the grocery store. "Here," I said, handing her six ones. "Go on over to the café and get something. If there's any change, I'd like it back."

She took the bills from me, but looked uncertain. "Have you eaten? At all?"

"Nah," I said, "I'm not hungry."

"That's not good, Stet," she said.

I laughed. "I won't act like a dad and you don't act like a mom, okay?"

"I'm serious!"

"So am I," I said again, picking up the wrench. She looked like she was ready to argue with me. "If you want to catch the lunch specials, you'd better get going fast. I'm sure they're almost over."

She took a few steps away and then turned back to me. "Can I come back here?"

"Sure," I said. "But this is all I'm doin'."

Kayla nodded and then disappeared around the corner. I called after her, "Be sure to shut and latch the gate behind you!"

"Okay!" she called back.

I was sure that I wouldn't see her again until I went home.

● ● ●

"Surprise!"

"Damnit!" I flinched instead of jumping this time, but I put enough torque on the wrench to strip the bolt.

"You don't sound happy to see me," Kayla pouted.

"I haven't seen you yet," I muttered, prying the bolt off. "I've only heard you—and it sounds like you're right behind me."

"I am."

"You know, maybe if you holler before you get right behind me, you wouldn't scare me so bad."

"Don't tell me you're scared of little old me," she laughed. "Can you stop long enough to eat?"

"What are you doing?" I asked, irritated. I didn't understand why she kept playing cutesy with me.

"I brought you lunch."

I stopped and turned around, staring in disbelief. She was holding a brown bag and a soda out to me.

"You didn't have to do that," I said.

"I know." She grinned. "But it was easy, since it was your money."

I rolled my eyes. "Yeah, I guess that would make it easy."

"Here, before I forget." Somehow she managed to get her hand in the pocket of her miniskirt and pull out a couple of coins. "Your change."

"Thanks." It wasn't a word I was used to saying.

"Come on," she said, pulling up the old bucket seats. "Take five for food."

"With service like this, I think I'll take ten," I said. I sat down and stretched my legs out. "Ooohh, maybe I'll take twenty."

She laughed as she opened her can of diet soda, and for a moment she almost seemed like any teenage girl.

"What'd you get me?"

"A turkey sub."

"Everything on it?" I lifted the top of the bun and took a peek.

"Yep."

I started to pick the onions off.

"You don't like onions?"

"How'd you guess?"

"What else don't you like?" she asked as she took a big bite of her sub.

"Green peppers," I said as I pulled them off.

"Is that it?"

"Pretty much." The first bite of sandwich seemed to melt in my mouth.

"I don't like onions either."

I was too busy eating to respond to that.

"Or green peppers. The only other thing I really don't like is fish."

"All fish?"

She nodded over her sub.

"Not even shellfish like crab or lobster?"

"I've never had them, so I don't know for sure, but I'd guess I don't like them."

"Me either," I said, and she grinned.

We finished our sandwiches quickly, but for some reason I wasn't in a hurry to get back to work. "So where'd you go this mornin'?"

Kayla shrugged as she stuffed her sandwich wrapping into the bag. "Around."

"Around? Around where? There's not a lot to do around here."

"You got that right," she said, then she sighed. "I ended up at the mill."

"What'd you do there?"

"Nothin', really. Just watched all the guys in their dirty work suits and grimy faces sit around and have a last smoke before goin' in to work."

"You saw the town's elite."

"I guess. There were a lot of guys there that looked real young." Her voice made it a question.

"Half of 'em were probably only a couple years older than you."

"But you're not down there." It sounded like another question.

"Don't want to be."

"You're gonna graduate."

"Yep."

"Then what?"

"I don't know yet. But somethin' better than the mill."

She laughed. "That won't take much."

"You learn quick."

"So if the guys around here go to the mill—"

"The girls marry the mill workers." I finished for her.

"Isn't that a little old-fashioned?"

"That's us, just a little old-fashioned town," I said, thinking of Vicky and Tony. "I guess the information superhighway has just done a bypass right over us."

Kayla laughed. "At least you've heard of the Internet."

"Be careful who you say that to. You tell the wrong person and I might be arrested for spying."

Kayla laughed again. She had a beautiful laugh. "Do you spend much time on the computer?"

I raised my eyebrows at her. "You haven't seen the office at our wonderful home?" She shook her head at me and I continued, "No, I only get on the computer when we have time at school. I don't know much." All they wanted us to do was word processing. I had had to teach myself graphics.

"Seriously, Stet, what do you want to do after graduation?"

"Seriously, I don't know." I did, though. I just didn't think I could do it. "What about you?"

"Assuming I survive another three and a half years of this and graduate?"

"Yeah."

She grinned and flipped her hair. "I want to be rich and famous, of course, sought after by gorgeous men."

"And how are you gonna do that?"

"I don't know," she said, and before I could say anything, she added, "maybe I'll be an actress, or a fashion designer. Maybe an artist."

"What kind of art?" She really had my attention now.

Uncomfortably, she shrugged. "Any kind."

"Can you draw freehand? Or do you just trace stuff?"

"I draw freehand. Why?"

"I need a design for my car," I said before I knew I was going to say it. "You want to help me come up with something?"

"A design?" she said skeptically. "Doesn't it come with one? You know, four wheels, an engine—"

"A *paint* design," I said.

"No, really?" she said, and I realized she was being sarcastic.

"Do you want to help or not?"

"I don't know, it might not fit into my busy schedule." I glared at her and she said quickly, "Of course I'd like to help. What do you want me to do?"

I got up and went to the toolbox, where I kept an

extra sketchbook. "These aren't very good," I explained. "My better book is at home."

"But it's locked in the shed and I can't get to it, right?" she asked, smiling.

I tried not to growl at her. "Anyway, you can see some of what I've done. I don't really like any of these, so feel free to start over."

"It's gonna be in color?" she asked, flipping through the pages.

"Yeah," I said. "But you can just do the basic design in pencil."

"Oh, I wasn't worried about that. I just wanted to know what colors I'm limited to."

"You're not," I said. "I haven't gotten the paints yet. And I'm going to airbrush it on, so I can do different shades of the same color pretty easily."

"Did you airbrush your shirts?" she asked.

"Yeah."

"They're pretty cool."

"Thanks."

Kayla tapped the sketchbook for a moment. "If I come up with a design you like, will you make a shirt for me?"

I grinned. "Absolutely."

"Then we have a deal," she said. "Where's the pencil?"

CHAPTER NINE

"ARE YOU done yet?"

I blinked and looked over at Kayla. Suddenly I realized it was almost twilight.

"No," I said, pushing myself out from under the hood. "But I think it's past quittin' time."

"Good," she said, standing up and stretching. "I've been ready to go for ages."

"You could have gone." I instantly regretted my words. Her face took on the hard look that she wore too often. "But I'm glad you stayed," I finished lamely.

"Yeah, like you even noticed my company."

I couldn't say anything to that, so instead I asked, "Did you come up with any designs for me?"

She shrugged. "A couple of things, but I don't know if you'll like any of them."

"Let's see." I held out my hand for the sketchbook.

"No." She shook her head. "I'm not done with them yet."

"Come on, just let me take a peek!"

"No!" she said, folding the book protectively between her arms and chest. "Not till I'm ready."

"Okay, okay, fine. Be that way."

"I will!" she retorted.

"I know," I smiled at her. It took a few seconds, but she finally relaxed and grinned back.

"So what are we doing tonight?"

"I was gonna stop at the grocery store." I began putting my tools away.

"Good," she said, nodding emphatically.

"And then I was gonna go home and work on my car."

She wrinkled her nose. "But you've been working on cars all day!"

"Not *my* car."

"Is there a difference?"

"Oh, yeah," I said as I stashed the toolbox. "For one thing, I'm puttin' mine together, not takin' it apart."

"Well, duh!"

"You're the one who asked if there's a difference!"

Kayla made a face at me. "What I meant was, working on cars is working on cars. It's *work*. It's not *fun*."

"It is for me," I said as we began to walk toward the front gate.

"This is what you do for fun?"

"Yeah."

"You don't do anything else?"

"Well—"

"Well what? What else do you do?"

"I used to go to the arcade a lot."

"That's for junior high kids," she said, waving it away.

"Maybe that's why I don't go anymore," I said dryly.

"What else?"

"Ummm . . . "

"Come on, Stet. You can't seriously expect me to believe that all you do is work on cars."

"Why not?"

I unwrapped the chain and she stepped through the

gate. I followed her, then rewrapped and locked it. She was staring at me the whole time. "That's really all you do?"

"That's really it."

"How sad."

"Why?" I asked as we started walking again.

"It's just so . . . limiting."

I cocked an eyebrow at her. "Why do I feel like I'm about to be the next topic on a talk show?"

She blushed a little, but didn't say anything.

I thought about my friends who were working at the mill and would never graduate. I thought about Tony, already married with a baby at eighteen. I thought about Vicky, stuck with a husband who didn't come home. I thought about my father, who couldn't go a day without a six-pack. "I don't find it limiting," I said quietly.

"Oh, I don't mean to insult you," she said quickly. "I just think it's sad that you're not just being a kid. Playing and having fun. Doing stupid things because you can."

I looked at her out of the corner of my eye. "And you are?"

"Are what?"

"Just being a kid."

"I take every chance I get."

"What do you consider kid things?"

"I don't know—doing things without taking responsibility for them. Not worrying about tomorrow. Just enjoying the moment."

"No," I said, "I guess I've never just been a kid."

"You mean you can't just be a kid anymore."

"No," I said, opening the grocery store door, "I mean I

didn't get to be at all." I grabbed a shopping cart and pulled out a thin stack of coupons. I gave her about a third of them. She didn't know the store as well as I did. "Find and get these. Don't get anything else. This is all I can afford right now. Meet me back by line two when you're done."

I was glad she turned quickly to go look for the stuff. I don't think I could have taken the stunned look on her face much longer.

When we met back by the register, her face had at least regained its normal expression. She put her items in the cart with mine.

"Coupons?" I asked.

She leafed through them quickly, pulled one out, and then handed them to me. When I raised an eyebrow, she shrugged a little. "The generic kind was cheaper than the name brand, even with the coupon."

I smiled. "Thanks."

"I lived on coupons with Mom, too," she said, not looking at me. "But at least she bought and paid for the food."

I nodded. She did such a good job of acting spoiled that I kept forgetting she wasn't.

As the guy at the register rang up our order, I tried not to hold my breath. I got lucky, though. This week I didn't have to choose an item or two to put back. I was able to pay for all of it, and even got seventy-two cents change.

I pushed the cart to the edge of the parking lot, and then handed Kayla two bags to carry. I took the other three.

"How long until you get paid again?"

"Don't know."

"You don't know? Don't you have a regular payday?"

"Not really. Jason just pays me when he can. It depends on how much work I've done and how much stuff he's sold. He'll probably pay me this weekend sometime."

"Oh."

We were quiet for a while. Finally I couldn't stand it. "Hey, cheer up! At least there will be stuff in the fridge now."

"For a few days," she said glumly. "Where do you think I could get a job?"

At first I almost told her she didn't need one, but then thought better of it. "I don't know. What can you do?"

"Not much," she admitted with half a laugh.

"You ever worked before?"

"No. I've never even baby-sat."

"I'm sure there's some kind of beginner job you could do."

"Yeah?" She looked up at me, using those big brown eyes again.

"Yeah," I said.

"Will you help me find one?"

"Sure," I said, even though I didn't want to. What I wanted was to let her just be a kid forever.

"'Kay," she said. We walked the rest of the way to the trailer in a comfortable silence.

● ● ●

"From now on, make sure you turn the lights off when you leave," I was saying to Kayla as we came in the front door.

"I did," she said at the same time a voice from the couch said, "I turned them on."

I stared in disbelief at Dad, then did a quick scan of the

trailer. "You bring home another kid?"

"No, smart-ass, I didn't. You two are more than enough."

I took the groceries to the kitchen and began putting them away. Kayla followed me, and to my surprise, so did Dad.

He leaned against the counter, watching us. Kayla tried to help. At first I spent more time giving her directions than putting anything away. I finally told her to just put stuff wherever there was room, which was pretty much every cabinet.

"So what are you doin' home?" I asked, when Dad continued to just stand there drinking beer.

"Thought we'd go out for dinner," he said casually, like it was something we did all the time. "Anybody hungry?"

"I'm starving," Kayla said quickly.

"Stet?"

"I'm not that hungry."

Kayla turned to me quickly. It was easy to read the 'please don't leave me with him' message in her eyes.

"You gonna go to MacGregor's?" I asked.

"Yep."

I met Kayla's eyes and shook my head. I wouldn't spend time there, not even for her. "No thanks."

"Suit yourself. Someday you'll learn not to turn down a free meal. Looks like you and me, kid," he said to Kayla as he shoved off the counter. "Let's get goin'. Two-for-one happy hour ends at seven."

Kayla followed him, and shot me one more pleading look before the door closed behind her.

I almost followed them. In fact, I got out the door and

didn't quite know which direction I was going to turn. I turned toward the shed. I couldn't go to MacGregor's. Too many of my old friends would be there. Most likely, Tony would be there, and he would probably have some girl other than Vicky on his arm.

My familiar old dusty shed provided me some comfort, but I still felt uneasy. For the next three hours, I got the shed ready for the painting. I pulled my car out and lay down the heavy plastic before I pulled it back in. Then I swept the plastic, and even went over it with a damp cloth, picking up all the dirt. I hung sheets of plastic over the walls and ceiling, overlapping them so that the interior of the shed would be dirt and dust free.

The only panel I couldn't secure was the one over the door. I worried about that, but there was nothing I could do. I would just have to make sure no one came in while I was painting, or right after I was done.

Finally, I went back to the trailer. Kayla and Dad were still gone. I fell asleep on the couch. I never heard anyone come in.

CHAPTER TEN

THE RINGING phone woke me. It was still dark, and for a few seconds I couldn't figure out what was making the sound. When I finally realized it was the phone, it was on the sixth or seventh ring.

"Screw it," I muttered, laying back down. By the time I got up, whoever it was would have hung up.

The phone rang twice more, then stopped.

I just had time for a huge yawn before it started ringing again.

This time I got up, ready to chew out whoever it was. "What do you want?" I demanded as I picked up the phone.

"Stet?"

"Kayla?"

"Yeah, um, could you please come pick me up?"

"Where are you?" I flipped on the light in the kitchen and winced in temporary blindness. When I could focus again, I saw that it was nearly four.

"I'm at the café," she whispered. "I don't want to walk home alone."

I didn't say anything. My mind still wasn't awake, and I didn't quite understand what was going on.

"Please, Stet," she said again, and I could tell she was crying. "Please don't make me walk home alone."

"Okay, okay, I'll be there. Hang tight."

"Thank you," and for some reason she started crying

harder. "Oh, thank you."

I hung up the phone and shook my head a few times, trying to get my brain working. Then I went out the front door, going straight to the shed.

● ● ●

I pulled up right in front of the door and tapped the horn lightly. A couple of truckers sitting at the diner's counter turned and glanced at me, but that was all. In the bright white light, I thought I saw Kayla sitting back at the last booth. I tapped the horn again. This time the waitress peered out the window at me, but Kayla didn't move.

I left the motor running, and hopped out of the car. I pulled the door open just enough to stick my head in. Yep, that was Kayla in the last booth.

"Kayla! Come on!" I only waited long enough to see her look up from her cup before I ran back out to my car. I wasn't about to let anyone take off with it or write me a ticket.

A few seconds later, Kayla came out. She stopped and looked around uncertainly. Impatient, I leaned over and opened the Civic's door. She stared at me as if she had never laid eyes on me before.

"Come on," I said. "I'm losing enough sleep as it is."

She climbed into my car. "It runs?" she said in shock.

"You're welcome. No, really, it's no trouble to wake from a dead sleep to come get you in the middle of the night."

"Thank you, Stet. I thought I already said that."

I turned the car around and waited impatiently for the light to change, scanning nervously for cops. I couldn't afford to get their attention.

"I just didn't know it ran."

I shook my head.

"I'm sorry," she said. "I didn't mean it the way it sounded. I didn't expect you so soon. I thought we'd be walking."

"You will be if you keep insultin' my car."

"I'm sorry," she repeated.

The light changed, and we pulled away from the other cars quickly.

"So what happened?" I asked. "You look like hell."

She really did. Her mascara had streaked down her face, and her eyes were bloodshot. Her hair, which she had been keeping so neatly pulled back from her face, was tousled. She stunk of cigarettes and beer.

"Dad and I had dinner, and then we hung out at the bar for a while. Did you know they'll serve anyone there?"

I nodded impatiently. I had known that since fifth grade.

"Anyway, I was havin' a really good time with these guys, and they invited me out to a party."

I could feel myself tensing all over. I couldn't wait for her to just tell the story. "Did they hurt you?" I asked through my teeth.

"No!" She sounded so surprised that I was able to relax.

"So what did happen?"

"I'm tellin' you, okay? So I went to this party, and it was okay, but it wasn't anythin' great. I mean, the bar was just as much fun. But this one guy, he and I were really hit-tin' it off. Then the next thing I know, he's gone, and everybody else is, like, passed out. So I decide I'll just walk back to the bar and get Dad. I didn't think it was that far. But I got all confused in the dark—"

"It didn't help that you're drunk," I muttered, fuming. How could Dad have let her leave without him?

"I am not! I only had one beer at the bar." Her voice dropped. "I just got really scared. I don't know how long I walked before I finally found the café. And I thought that I'd just, you know, get myself together and walk home from there. But I didn't like the way the guys at the counter were looking at me, and I didn't want to get lost again, so I called you." She wiped her eyes with her hands, smearing the mascara even more. "I'm sorry, I really am. But I was just so scared."

"It's okay," I said as we pulled into the shed.

We got out of the car and I made a face.

"What? What's wrong?"

"Nothin'," I said as I pulled the big door shut and locked it, "I'm just gonna have to spend a couple more hours tomorrow, cleaning the floor again," I nodded to the dirty tire tracks on the plastic.

Kayla looked around. "What's all this for?"

"Paintin'."

"You gonna start soon?"

"Hope to. As soon as I've got a design, that is." I looked at her. "Do you have anything yet?"

"I'm working on it," she said. "Give me some time. Why do you have to clean the floor again?" she asked. "Isn't the plastic just gonna get dirty anyway?"

"It'll catch paint, sure. But I don't want any *dirt* in here. If it gets stirred up, it'll get stuck in the paint."

"Oh," she said, nodding. I could tell she wasn't sure

what I was talking about, but I was too tired to care.

"Come on," I said.

She scurried to the trailer while I locked the padlock. By the time I got to the living room couch, the door to my bedroom was already shut.

● ● ●

I meant to get up early the next day, I really did. But for some reason, my internal clock wasn't set right.

What woke me was a loud thump. I sat up and turned toward the noise. Kayla was looking at me with an anxious grimace.

"I'm sorry," she said, "I didn't mean to wake you."

"'S all right," I said, scratching my head. "What was that?"

"I bumped the cabinet door and it shut kind of hard."

I nodded, still scratching my head. Then I realized how bright it was. "What time is it?"

"Nearly ten."

"Oh—" I got up quickly, cursing.

"What's wrong?"

"I'm late," I muttered, starting down the hall.

"For what?"

"Work." I went into my room, grabbed some clean clothes, and turned to go to the bathroom. I nearly ran Kayla over. I hadn't realized she had followed me.

"Do you really have to go again today?"

"Yeah."

"Why?"

"Kayla, it's my job. It's how I get paid. It's how we eat."

"Who pays you?"

For a minute I just stared at her. "My boss."

"How's he gonna know you're late getting in? Or early leavin'?"

"He's got a clock."

"But is he ever there?"

"Oh," I said, suddenly understanding. "Yeah, he's usually there. He wasn't yesterday 'cause he's sick. He'll probably be in today."

"Oh," Kayla said. That was it.

I waited patiently for three more seconds, then said, "Do you mind?"

"What? Oh," she said again, blushing as she moved so I could get into the bathroom. But she didn't leave.

I started to shut the door, but then stopped. "What's up, Kayla?"

"Huh? Oh, nothin'," she finally seemed to realize that she was just standing in the hallway, and she turned and went back to the kitchen.

I shut the door and took a fast shower. When I came back out, she was already gone.

●　●　●

The salvage yard gates were wide open when I got there. I walked toward the office, but stopped when a voice in the little engine row called out, "You're late."

"And a good mornin' to you! Glad to see you're feeling better," I said, walking over to him. Jason looked like hell. The black patch practically leapt off his pale, drawn face, and his eye was bloodshot. He still looked like he might fall over.

Jason grunted at me. He picked up a lawn-mower engine, but then set it back down. Or rather, he dropped it.

"What are you doing here?"

"I own the place, remember?"

"You ought to be at home. Or at the doctor's." I paused, taking a look at him. "Or maybe at a funeral home, making some arrangements."

"I said you're late, not funny."

"I stayed late last night, too."

"Not 'ccordin' to the books."

Instead of giving Jason a rip for that, I took a deep breath. He really wasn't feeling well, I reminded myself. "I didn't bother opening the office at all yesterday. I—"

"You left us shut yesterday?" Jason demanded.

"I don't have register keys, remember? You didn't give 'em to me. I didn't want people comin' in if I couldn't sell stuff."

Jason scowled.

"Since I didn't open the office," I continued, "I didn't sign in or out."

"Since you didn't sign in or out, I don't think I'll pay you. Especially since you kept us shut down."

I just stared at him.

He looked away after a few seconds and said, "What work did you get done?"

I told him and I could tell he was impressed with the amount of work I had finished. He tried to hide it though. "I'll credit you for four hours," he grumbled.

"Jason, I worked nearly nine hours yesterday."

"Then you was bein' lazy, since you didn't finish all the cars."

"You know I'm not lazy. You've always taken my word before."

Jason fiddled with his eye patch. "I'll give you

four hours," he repeated. "That's it."

"Why're you tryin' to pick a fight with me?"

He ignored me. "You better get to work on those cars. I expect you to keep the yard open tomorrow while I'm gone, and you won't have time to strip cars *and* help people find what they need." He turned around and walked back to the office.

I stared after him for a few moments, but then just turned and went to the row of cars waiting to be dismantled.

I worked for hours, in the quiet, the way I always did. My mind, though, was anything but quiet.

Something was wrong with Jason. That was my first concern. He had always been there for me with a pat on the back or a kick in the butt, depending on what I needed. Now I thought he needed a pat on the back or a little help. But he was trying to make me kick him in the butt.

He'd be gone for the weekend, which meant I wouldn't be able to find out what was wrong for a few days. Plus, I wouldn't be able to help him out as much any more because of the stupid school contract. I hated that more than anything.

I was scared about school now. Could I really make it? I usually did okay work, but I missed a lot. And most of my teachers got tired of giving me make-up work and would just excuse the assignments I had missed. Now I was gonna have to do them all. I had to graduate.

Thinking about Kincaid's suggestion that I get my GED made me mad. I could graduate, I knew I could. I was just going to have to stay out of trouble. Which meant no more pranks for money. Without money from my pranks, less money from my job, and a sister to support, I would probably lose a few pounds in the next eight months, unless I sold a lot more T-shirts.

And then there was Kayla. All nice and sweet one minute, then a drunken snot the next. I didn't think either of those were the real Kayla—they seemed to be just an act for my benefit. I wondered how long it would take until she would just be herself.

My thoughts were a whirlwind that drove time by. When I finally decided I had to get something to drink, it was mid-afternoon.

I walked around the office to the spigot. For several minutes, I sat next to it, either dunking my head under it or just drinking out of it. Finally I decided I had taken a long enough break, and I headed back to the cars. As I passed the office, though, I heard something that made me stop.

I stuck my head in the door, and was amazed to see Jason sitting behind the counter and Kayla leaning on the other side, both of them laughing. They stopped as soon as they saw me.

"Hey, what's going on?"

They exchanged guilty looks. "Nothin'," Kayla declared.

"I ain't heard either of you laugh like that ever before. Somethin's goin' on."

"Jason was—"

"Your sister—" they both began at the same time, then stopped, laughing again.

"Glad I don't have to introduce you," I said while they collected themselves.

"Your sister has offered you an alibi."

"For what?"

"For being here yesterday and today."

"I don't need an alibi for that."

"What he means is I told him how long you were here yesterday, and why you were late today," Kayla explained.

"I don't need an alibi for that," I repeated.

"I'll give you the full nine hours for yesterday," Jason said.

"Good. But I don't see why you wouldn't just take my word." That pissed me off more than him threatening not to give me the credit.

Kayla didn't know I was upset. She grinned at me. "Hungry?"

"No," I began, but then stopped. "Yeah, actually."

Jason reached down behind the counter and opened the mini-fridge behind it. Then he set a brown bag on the counter. "She brought you lunch. Why, after the way you've been treatin' her, I'm sure I don't know."

"Thanks," I said to Kayla as I picked up the bag.

"Don't forget his soda," she said to Jason.

Jason muttered something and then reached under the counter for the soda.

"So where'd you go this morning?" I asked, opening the bag. She had packed me two sandwiches and a small baggie of crackers.

She shrugged. "Out for a walk."

"Didn't you get enough of that last night?"

"I don't want to talk about it," she said stiffly.

"Why not? If it was good enough to get me up for, it's got to be good enough to talk about."

She shook her head. Jason spoke up. "Lay off, Stet. You don't pick on people who bring you lunch."

"No," I retorted, "I just pick on them when they wake me at four in the morning for a ride."

"I said I was sorry!" Kayla wailed.

"I said lay off!" Jason growled.

I glared at him. "Why are you on her side? I thought you were my friend."

"I am. And friends tell each other when they're being idiots. So shut up."

"Well, as a friend, I'm telling you that you've been a jerk lately."

Jason's good eye stared at me. "I think you've taken a long enough break."

"Too long," I agreed. I picked up the soda and threw the last of the crackers and bag away. I had my hand on the office door when Kayla spoke up.

"What time will you be home?"

"Later," I said, and walked out the door.

I walked back to the cars, but it wasn't easy. All I wanted to do was leave. I wanted to leave absolutely everything. Just start walking down that highway and see where it took me. But everything and everyone I ever knew was here.

I grimly set to work on the truck, and stripped three bolts before I decided I needed to cool down a little before continuing. Otherwise, I might snap something right in my hands.

I walked around the truck three times and then sat down in one of the discarded seats. I leaned my head back and closed my eyes.

"What the hell's the matter with you?" Jason demanded.

I didn't turn to look at him or even open my eyes. "Could ask you the same thing."

"No, I don't think you could. I'm not the one goin' around like somebody pissed on my shoes."

"No, you're just goin' around like some jerk who doesn't care about his friends anymore."

"I don't know what you're talkin' about—" Jason began.

"Oh yes you do," I said, and now I did open my eyes. He was standing right in front of me. "You've been feelin' all sick and stuff for a couple of months now—"

"I ain't said a word to you 'bout that!"

"Exactly."

We stared at each other for a few long moments.

"How'd you know I was sick?" he finally muttered.

I sighed. "How could I not know? You've been in a rotten mood. The only patch you've worn for three weeks now is your POW/MIA one. You've been my best friend for years now. And you've been shuttin' me out."

We were quiet again, but he wouldn't look at me.

"You're goin' to the city for a real doctor, huh?"

Jason glanced up in surprise. "How—? Yeah. I am."

"Must be somethin' serious."

"It ain't nothin'," he said gruffly. I didn't say anything, just raised my eyebrows. "Look, I don't want to talk 'bout it till I know what I'm up against, okay?"

"Okay," I said easily. "That's all you had to say. You didn't have to shut me out."

"Sorry," he said shortly. After a pause, he said, "So what's wrong with you? You ain't sick."

I laughed and shook my head. "No, I ain't sick. But I almost get kicked out of school, my sister suddenly shows up, and—"

"And what?"

"Nothin'."

"Come on, Stet. You can't shut me out either."

It took me a couple minutes to gather my thoughts. Jason just waited. Finally I blurted out. "Kayla shows up. She's an emotional mess. Dad don't have time to register her for school, but he's got time to take her out drinkin'. She's only fourteen, but that's never stopped nobody in this town. So she goes out to party, and I'm the one who's got to be there to pick her up. And then she comes here, and talks all pretty to you, and you believe her instead of me."

"You two was sayin' the same thing!"

"Yeah, but it took her sayin' it for you to believe it!"

"Stet, I'm sorry 'bout that," Jason almost looked embarrassed. "I was gonna give you the full hours, it's just that I was pissed that you came in late." He looked at me shrewdly. "I don't think that's everything."

"I don't want to talk about nothin' else."

"Stet," Jason said warningly.

"No, man. I'm done." How could I talk to him about something I didn't even understand? I had no idea what to make of my mother now. She had left me behind, without any explanation. And now I find it wasn't because she didn't want to be a mother.

And what about Dad? Why did he suddenly offer to take us out to dinner? He hadn't taken me out since elementary school. One minute he acted mad that he had another kid to deal with, the next he acted like he was proud of her and wanted to show her off. He hadn't tried to show me off for years.

"Kayla seems like a good kid," Jason said.

I shook my head again. "Don't go by first impressions," I said.

"Give her a chance. She's goin' through a tough time."

"Oh? Really? Thanks, I didn't catch that."

"I know you're goin' through a tough time too," he said. "But you've always been tough. You can handle it. She's gonna have to learn to be tough. She's gonna need help from you."

"It ain't fair," I said, not about Kayla, but about everything. Jason, as usual, understood what I didn't say.

"Nope," he said. "But it never is." He paused. "I need to run a couple errands. Be gone for a bit."

"Got it covered," I said. "Just shut the gate so people don't wander in on me. Unless you want me running the office."

"Nah. It'll be quiet this afternoon anyway." He was all business now. "You done anythin' with the Ford yet?"

"Nope. Probably tomorrow."

"Skip it. We'll offer it as is, unless someone comes in askin' for a certain part. Otherwise, ain't worth our time."

"Got it," I said, nodding. The Ford didn't have much body damage. It could bring in a decent price as a whole car that just needed some hours of sweat.

He turned and looked at the truck. "Ain't you done with that one yet?"

"Almost."

"Then get your butt in gear," he said, turning and heading back toward the office. "I want the truck done before you leave, and you're leaving tonight at six."

"Why?"

"'Cause I'm closin' up shop."

"So? I can lock up."

"I'll pay you tonight when you leave."

"You just paid me last week," I said suspiciously. "And if you want to pay me again, you can do it now."

"Stet, come by the office at six and sign out. You need some time off."

I knew that tone of voice. "Yessir," I said. I pushed myself up off the seat, and never noticed if he flipped me off or not.

CHAPTER ELEVEN

"STET!" JASON'S holler barely reached me. "Quittin' time!"

"Damnit," I muttered to myself before I hollered back, "Okay!" I had finished the truck an hour ago but hadn't gotten as far as I wanted to with the next car. I put my tools away and tossed the box in the new Beetle.

I headed back to the office, thinking that Jason must really not be feeling well if he wouldn't even walk out to get me. He always used that as an excuse to check on my progress.

The first person I saw when I walked in was Kayla. "Hey," I said in surprise.

"Hey," she said. She was grinning from ear to ear and practically glowing. Jason was standing behind her, and he was grinning bigger than I had ever seen.

"What's goin' on?"

"It's payday," Jason said, nodding his head toward the counter.

I turned and looked. Several gallons of metallic paint were on the counter. Two gallons of blue, two of brown, one gold, one black, and a couple of white. "What's all this?" I asked in confusion.

"It's for your car," Kayla began.

"I got the right kind, didn't I?" Jason sounded a little anxious. "I thought you said this was the brand you wanted."

"It is, it is," I said quickly. It was also the brand I couldn't afford. There was easily over one hundred dollars' worth of paint on the counter. "This is great," I said. slowly walking to the counter and hefting one of the cans. "I just don't understand."

"You're ready to paint, right?"

"Almost."

"The *car's* ready, right? You're just waitin' for an idea."

"Yeah."

Jason looked at Kayla expectantly. She just stood there and blushed. He gave her a little nudge, and she still didn't move. He put a hand firmly on her shoulder and pushed her forward. "Here," she said, in a little voice. "Jason's convinced you'll use it."

I took the sketchbook. When I opened the first page, I stared in amazement.

"It's a falcon," Kayla said quickly. "I was gonna do an eagle, but I thought that'd be silly on a little car."

I was speechless.

"You don't like it," Kayla said flatly. "I can do something else."

"Don't you dare," I said, finally finding my voice. "It's awesome!" She had sketched the car from the front and from the side. The hood of the car would be the falcon's head, with beak open, the side and door panels would have the talons and wings of the bird. I could almost hear the screams of rage and triumph coming from the falcon.

I looked up at Kayla. She was shifting uncertainly from one foot to the other. "You did this today?"

"Most of it. I've been fiddling with it ever since you gave me the sketchbook."

"You're really good."

"Thanks." She blushed even more. "Jason said you could do the details once you had the design. I'm sure you'll do a better job."

"I don't know about that," I said. "But I definitely want to use this."

"I've never worked with an airbrush, but I could help if you want."

I appreciated the offer, and I nodded, but didn't really know how to answer her. My car had been my private project. Once or twice a friend had come over to help, but seeing them with their hands on my car almost felt like a physical violation.

"You owe me," Kayla said smugly.

I tore my eyes off the sketch. "Huh?"

"You promised me a shirt."

"Yeah," I said, looking back at the book. "You bet."

Jason cleared his throat. "When're you gonna start?"

I gave a little grin. "After seeing this," I said, lifting the sketchbook, "I'm dying to start tonight. But since I've got to work here all weekend, I'll probably save it till next weekend." I didn't say anything about taking the time off, but I would have to. Once I started painting, I didn't want to stop till I was done.

"You gonna do it in that old shed?"

"Well, I can't do it in the middle of a field, so, yeah, that was my plan."

"Smart-ass," Jason said. "How're you gonna set the paint?"

Kayla looked a little confused, but I said slowly, "I was just gonna let it set for a few days at a time, make sure it takes."

"You want to use the space heaters?" he asked, gesturing to the two on the floor. "They might speed it along."

"Yeah," I said slowly, looking at them. It wouldn't be an oven like the professionals used, but it'd be a whole lot better than just letting it air-dry. "If you don't mind."

"I don't mind," he said. "And if you got it all set for your shed, I guess I won't offer my garage then."

I stared at him. "Seriously?"

"Why not? I've got to take my car into the city with me, so it'll be empty till Monday mornin'. If you start Saturday evening, you should be able to finish before the yard opens at noon on Sunday."

It would mean a weekend without sleep, but that was hardly anything new. Jason kept his garage clean, and it had the benefit of a cement floor and walls without holes. I wouldn't have to worry about blowing dirt.

"Jason, that would be too awesome," I said.

"You can say thank you any time," he said dryly.

"Thank you! Thank you! Thank you!" I said. I shook his hand and then hugged Kayla. "Thank you!"

"Well, come on then. Let's get these cans loaded into my car, and I'll leave 'em in my garage for you. And I'll give you two a lift home."

I was too overwhelmed to argue. We quickly had the paint in the car. Kayla climbed into the back seat, and I walked out and locked the gates after Jason pulled through. He dropped us off a few minutes later.

"Here're the keys for the weekend," he said before I got out.

"Any last-minute orders?"

"Sell everything you can, but don't give stuff away."

I grinned and climbed out of the car, holding the door open for Kayla. She turned and headed to the trailer. "Take good care of your sister," Jason said in a low tone as I pulled out the two space heaters. "She needs you right now."

"Yessir," I said. "You tell that doctor to fix you up so you can quit bein' a jerk."

"I'll quit bein' a jerk soon as you quit bein' a smart-ass." Jason said. "Now seriously, you be good."

I laughed, "Yessir."

In spite of our joking, I felt sad watching him drive away. As he pulled out of the trailer park, he honked. I picked up the heaters, turned, and walked over to the shed.

● ● ●

I had just finished sweeping the tire tracks off the plastic when the side door opened.

"Close the door!" I shouted.

Startled, Kayla closed the door quickly behind her, catching her ponytail in it. "What?" she asked, looking around nervously and stuck to the door. "What's wrong?"

"You're letting the dirt in," I complained.

She gave me an irritated look, then carefully inched the door open enough to release her ponytail. "I didn't think you were gonna do any painting tonight."

"I'm not. I'm gonna prime it."

"Prime it?"

"Put primer on it, so it will be ready to take the paint. It has to dry for at least twenty-four hours, so I need to do it now."

"How do you put primer on?"

"With the air compressor," I said, waving toward the airbrush.

"So it *is* painting."

"Well, yeah, in a way." I started pulling out newspapers and masking tape.

"Can I help?"

I looked over at her. "You don't want to go back to MacGregor's tonight?"

She shrugged. "Not really."

I tossed her a roll of tape.

"What do I do with this?"

"You help me tape up the windows."

She wrinkled her nose.

"Unless you want to just sit and watch."

Looking at the barren shed, she wrinkled her nose even more. "Where do we start?"

We started with the windshield. "Why don't you want to go to MacGregor's tonight?"

"I don't know."

"I thought you had a good time last night."

"Before I called you, yeah. But I don't know who I can trust over there."

I snorted. "No one."

"Why don't you hang out there?"

"Don't want to."

"I know *that*," she said. "But why? It seems like everyone from town goes there."

"I guess maybe that's my reason."

"And you don't drink."

"That too."

She was quiet for a moment, then she said slowly, "Is Dad an alcoholic?"

"What was your first clue?"

"So why doesn't he get help?"

"In his words, if it ain't broke, don't fix it. He likes his life the way it is. He doesn't see a problem with it."

"But you do."

"Yeah," I said, looking at her, "and it only took you one night to see a problem with it, too."

"Is that why you don't drink?"

"Sort of."

We had finished covering the windshield and passenger side window when suddenly she stopped. "Wait. How are we gonna get the car over to Jason's?"

"I was going to drive it, unless you have a better idea."

"How are you going to see to drive?"

"We'll take off all the paper and tape."

"Won't we have to do it all over again?"

"Well, yeah," I said sarcastically.

"So why don't we wait till we get to Jason's?"

"I told you, it takes twenty-four hours for the primer to set. So if I want to finish this weekend, I need to start now."

"Oh. Okay."

We went back to work, but I sensed she had another question. "Now what?"

"Well, why are you in such a hurry? I mean, it's been two years, right? What's another few days?"

"I won't get another chance to use Jason's garage," I began.

"I'm sure he'd let you," she cut in. "All you'd have to do is ask."

She was absolutely right, but I wasn't going to admit it. Instead I continued, "And, since it *has* been two years, I'd like to get it done. You know, be able to show it off and stuff."

"Well, I'm sure your friends have seen it, right? They know how cool it's gonna be."

Using the excuse of ripping off another piece of tape, I stayed quiet.

"Your friends have been helping, right?" she asked again as she secured the paper to the rear window.

"A couple of times."

"You mean you've done all this by yourself?"

"Pretty much." I got uncomfortable in her astonished stare. "What? It's no big deal."

"I thought guys used car time to hang out together and stuff."

"Sometimes," I said, thinking of when I first got the car. We were sophomores, and no one had a license or full-time job yet. Tony, Bill, and Chris had been over a lot, just talking about it, looking at it with big plans. But when time had come for the real work, the long hours and the tedious repetition, none of them were interested. They had all found future wives and a life at the mill.

"Stet?"

"Hmm?"

"Why don't you drink?"

"Kayla, I told you—"

"No you didn't! You told me Dad's part of the reason. You said, 'Sort of,' which means there's more."

"It's stupid."

"I bet it's not."

"Look, can we finish this first? I don't feel like talkin' when I work."

"Okay," she said. And to my surprise, she stayed quiet.

We finished the last window. I asked Kayla to set up the space heaters. "Go grab a couple of towels from the house first," I said, "and soak 'em in water."

"Okay," she said, and disappeared quickly from the shed. I smiled. She barely opened the door enough to squeeze her body out sideways. At least she learned quickly.

She was back a few minutes later with dripping towels. I was busy getting the airbrush ready for the primer. "Now what?"

"Go wring them out a little," I said. "We don't want to set electric heaters in a puddle!"

"Well you didn't tell me what I was gonna do with 'em!" She was back in the shed in a few moments. "So I just set the heaters on these, right?"

"Yeah. Make sure you're close enough to the outlets."

"What are they for?

"Hopefully to keep the heaters from melting through the plastic."

"Oh. How are you goin' to keep 'em damp for twenty-four hours?"

"I don't know," I admitted.

"Sounds like a job I could do," she said.

I grinned. "Thanks, that would be great." The airbrush was ready. I looked around, then picked up two bandanas. "Here," I said, tossing her a faded green one.

She looked at me strangely, but then put it around her head, covering her mouth and nose. "You know it's really not my color," she said, brown eyes peering at me.

I laughed. "Okay. Now, we can't open that door till

after I'm done, so if you need to go use the girls' room, now's the time."

"I'm ready," she said.

I had just turned on the compressor when the shed door was suddenly flung open. Kayla and I both turned and shouted "Shut the door!" as my father came in.

Scratching at his beer gut, my father looked around. "What the hell happened in here?" he asked, poking at the plastic hanging from the wall.

I reached over and turned off the compressor. "Shut the door!" I yelled again.

"I'm not stayin', don't worry," he said. "Just want to know if you're comin' with me tonight," he said to Kayla.

"No thanks," she said, "I think I'll stay here."

"What for?"

"Will you shut the damn door!" I yelled again. I wanted to beat something, but the only two things close enough were my car and the compressor, and I couldn't afford to damage either of them.

"I'll leave my shed door open if I please," Dad sneered at me.

Kayla got up, went around Dad, and shut the door.

"Thank you!"

"You know, Stet, you're just wound too tight. You may get out of here someday, but that don't mean nothin'. You'll still just be a hick like me. But you'll be a hick nobody likes, 'cause you don't know how to talk to people and be with people."

"Shut up," I said. It was the first time in years I had bothered to respond to one of my father's comments. But I was so sick of him.

"What did you say?"

"I said—"

"Hey, Dad, let's go."

I stared at Kayla. She was tugging on his arm.

"I thought you said you weren't comin' tonight," Dad said, looking at her suspiciously.

"Well, I wasn't. But Stet don't really need me around anymore, right?" She pulled the bandana off and dropped it on the floor.

"You can stay," I began weakly.

"Yeah, but you don't *need* me. Come on," she said, tugging his arm again. "Let's get out of here."

He gave a short nod. "Glad you got some sense. At least you know how to enjoy life while it's here." He pushed the door wide open. I winced as I saw a cloud of dust and a small tumbleweed blow in.

"Kayla," I tried. She turned and winked at me, and then disappeared. The door shut firmly behind her.

I sighed and went looking for the tumbleweed. I found it, and quickly put it back outside. Then I set to work with the compressor. It only took me a few hours to do the whole car, but those hours took forever. I thought I'd never finish. The shed, my escape and comfort for years, was cold and lonely that night.

● ● ●

When I woke up, I was on the lumpy couch. I had actually walked down to MacGregor's the night before, but I couldn't make myself cross the parking lot and go in. Instead, I had walked back home, sat on the couch, and watched stupid TV shows until I had fallen asleep. Sometime during the night I had gotten up to turn it off, but that was all I remembered. I didn't remember hearing anyone come in.

The first thing I did was go out to the shed and check on the heaters. The towels were completely dry, but at least they hadn't caught fire and the plastic wasn't melting. I walked slowly around the Civic. I couldn't see any dirt or bubbles in the primer. Hopefully I wouldn't see any tonight, either.

I ran the towels into the kitchen and got them wet again. After I replaced them, I locked the shed and went back to the trailer. Dad's bedroom door was open and his messed-up bed was empty. The door to my room was closed.

As quietly as I could, I eased the door open. Peering through the darkness, I could barely make out the tousled hair on the pillow. I tiptoed to my dresser, pulled out some clean clothes, and tiptoed back to the door. Halfway there, I froze in my tracks as Kayla turned in her sleep.

"Stetson's my brother. Do you know him?"

I grinned. She was talking in her sleep.

"Will you let me drive? I've always . . . " her voice trailed off into mumbles.

Carefully I closed the door behind me. *She must really be dreaming if she thinks I'll let her drive my car,* I thought as I went to take my shower.

When I came out, she was still asleep. I left her a note on the counter, asking her to check the towels in the shed if she got the chance and inviting her to drop by the salvage yard later. Then I went off to work.

CHAPTER TWELVE

"YOU SURE he didn't tell you?"

"Sorry, Nick. He didn't say a thing. But I won't sell it to anyone this weekend, if you want to talk to him about it first."

Nick Arnot, one of the cheapest regulars we had, spat off to one side. "No, I need the part now. I'll just keep the receipt and he and I can hash it out later. When'd you say he'll be back?"

"Monday," I said, hoping I was right. I missed Jason. Working the register and keeping track of who was trying to take what wasn't any fun. Nick was trying to convince me that Jason had promised him the whole distributor cap and wires for only five bucks. I wasn't real worried about Nick harassing Jason about it later. Nick was just trying to push me around.

I turned my attention back to the weed whacker in front of me, but not for long. The office door opened again and I set my screwdriver down, trying not to growl in frustration. I hated it when my work was interrupted.

"Whaddya need?" I asked, turning around.

"Something to do in this podunk town!" Kayla said.

I laughed.

She surveyed the office. "Doin' a lot of business?"

I shrugged. "There are people walking around the yard. Stuff's moving."

Kayla nodded kind of absently and walked over to one

of the repaired washing machines. She took off her dark glasses and began fiddling with the knobs.

"How was last night?"

"All right." She didn't turn around and her voice was flat.

"That good, huh?"

With her back still to me she shrugged.

"Kayla? What's up?"

She sighed, put her glasses back on, and came over to lean against the counter. Now she was fiddling with the jar of pens. "This is one dull town."

"Yeah," I said, watching her carefully. "How drunk did you get last night?"

"Not at all."

"Don't lie."

"I'm not!"

In one quick motion I reached across the counter and ripped off her glasses, expecting to expose her bloodshot eyes. "My God, what happened?" Her left eye was black and swollen shut.

"Gimme those!" she hissed, tearing them out of my hands and shoving them back on her face. "I have them on for a reason."

"I noticed. What happened?"

"I'd really rather not talk about it."

"Too bad. Start talking."

Even through the glasses I could feel the glare she gave me. "Does the phrase 'none of your business' mean anything to you?"

"Nope."

"I just had a misunderstanding with someone at MacGregor's."

"Keep going."

"That's it. Really."

"Kayla . . . "

She muttered something I couldn't hear. I just stared at her. "It looks worse than it is. It's no big deal, really."

"Then quit stalling and just tell me."

"We were dancing. That's all I wanted to do. And then . . . " she shook her head.

"Then what?" My stomach was twisting around like a snake.

"He started doin' stuff, and he wouldn't stop when I told him to. So . . . "

She drifted off again and I nearly screamed with frustration. It must have shown on my face, 'cause she blurted the rest out really fast.

"Then, I don't know, somehow I managed to push him away from me, but I must have pushed too hard or something, because all of a sudden I ran into one of the posts."

I raised my eyebrows. "Seriously?"

She squirmed a little uncomfortably, and began to flush.

"Kayla? What aren't you telling me?"

Grinning in a bashful way, she said, "I kind of, um, kneed him and that's when he shoved me away."

"Oh." I had to grin. "Good for you. But, you know, maybe . . . Never mind."

"What?" She asked.

"Nothing."

"Uh-uh. No way. You make me talk, you better talk too!"

I shifted uncomfortably and traced a pattern on the countertop. "Maybe you should think about wearing . . . I don't know, stuff that isn't, well . . . so . . . "

I could feel her glare again and didn't dare look up at her.

After a couple of long seconds, she said, "Did it ever occur to you that maybe I don't like the things I wear?" Her voice was shaking slightly. "That maybe I wear them because they're all I have to wear? That maybe these clothes are all a couple years old and I've grown a little?"

I closed my eyes tightly and lifted my head before opening them to see the angry tears in her eyes. "Kayla, I'm sorry. That was really stupid of me."

She didn't say anything.

"I'm really sorry," I said, wanting to put my hand on hers, but afraid to. "Who was the guy?" I asked, trying to find something else to talk about.

She shrugged. "I don't remember his name."

"Kayla," I warned.

"Look, you don't need to go gettin' all brotherly. He was dealt with. Let it go."

"You tryin' to protect me or him?"

"Neither. Both. It wasn't a big deal," she repeated. "Just let it go."

"So other than gettin' groped and then gettin' a shiner, you had a nice evening?"

"It was better than I expected," she said, taking her glasses off and leaning forward on the counter. "Dad actually talked to me. Not much, but some."

"Oh?" I turned back to the weed whacker. "'Bout what?"

"You, mostly."

I dropped the screwdriver and looked at her. "What?"

"He told me that you're going to be the first in the family to graduate from high school. I told him I'm going to be the second, as long as he gets me registered."

"What'd he say to that?" I picked the screwdriver back up and started working again.

"He called me a smart-ass and then promised to be there Monday morning to sign the papers."

"Good for you."

"He misses you."

The screwdriver slipped and sliced my finger a little. I popped my finger in my mouth and stared at her. She was watching me carefully. I said, "He doesn't miss me. I'm home more than he is. And he's practically counting down the days till I graduate and move out."

Kayla shook her head. "I don't think so."

"What'd he say to make you think that?" I asked, facing her and putting my elbows on the counter.

"Nothing sp—"

"He didn't say anything about me. You're just trying to turn this into some sort of fairy tale instead of the reality."

"What reality is that?"

"We were born to alcoholic trailer trash." She looked down at the counter, but not before I saw the hurt in her eyes. I kept forgetting how young she was. "And we're going to graduate, stay sober, and get out of this podunk town."

She looked up at me, smiling but not convinced.

"We'll look out for each other. Okay?"

"Yeah."

A couple of guys came in looking for parts, and I went out to help them. Around one, Kayla took my keys and went home to check the heaters and shower. At four she came back, with sandwiches and chips. We just kicked around that last hour, talking and playing tic-tac-toe. I was also working on some new shirt designs.

"Tell me something good about Mom."

"That's not easy."

"Try."

"Umm ... " she crunched on a chip for a minute. "When I was little, she used to tell me bedtime stories while brushing my hair."

I grinned. "I can picture you sitting in front of her, holding the book open—"

"Oh, there wasn't a book," Kayla said. "Mom made the stories up. They were about—" Suddenly her eyes opened wide. "Oh my God, I can't believe I forgot!"

"What?"

"I was always a princess—"

"No wonder you've got such an attitude," I said.

Kayla glared at me and continued, "And sometimes there was a prince. His name was Stetson."

I snapped the pencil in half. "You're lying."

"I'm not."

"I thought you said she never mentioned me."

"She didn't. Not as my brother."

We were both quiet for a few minutes, finishing our sandwiches and thinking. I didn't know how to feel about Mom making me a prince in the stories even though I was the one who needed rescuing.

"Your turn. Tell me something good about Dad."

"You mean other than the fact that taking a teenage girl to a bar and buying her drinks is more important than registering her for school?"

Kayla rolled her eyes at me. "Yes. Other than that."

"He's always been busy with work," I said slowly. "Making sure we had enough to pay bills."

"I thought you paid for everything."

I shook my head as I spun the soda can in my hands. "He used to pay for the groceries. And even an occasional night at the diner. It wasn't until I was in junior high that he started spending all his time at the bar, started—"

"Started what?"

"That's when he started ragging me, picking on me for all my dreams and plans."

"Well, that's better than what I've seen," she said doubtfully, "but I'm not sure it qualifies as good."

"You're right," I said. "Hmm, something good. We sometimes played ball during halftime, and he taught me how to play poker. I know!" I sat up in the booth. "He took me fishing once."

"Big deal."

"It was a big deal," I insisted.

"Because?" Kayla raised her eyebrows, encouraging me.

"Because he took two days off. And it was just us, none of his drinking buddies. In fact, he didn't even drink while we were gone. We just hung out, and sang campfire songs, and took naps in the afternoon. . . . " I shook my head. It was the most relaxing and fun time I remembered ever having in my life.

"How long ago was this? How old were you?"

I frowned. "I was probably eight."

"Mom stopped telling me stories when I was seven."

We both sat silently, thinking about parents we didn't understand, or even know.

CHAPTER THIRTEEN

THAT NIGHT was awesome. I closed up the yard at five, just like always, although the temptation to close early was incredible. If it hadn't been for the fact that the primer needed the full twenty-four hours to dry, I probably would have blown out of there around three.

We walked home together, and got clothes and things to take with us over to Jason's.

"Now you're sure you want to come, right?" I asked.

Her face clouded over. "If you don't want me—"

"No, no, that's not it. It's just that Jason lives a lot further away from the salvage yard, and we're gonna have to leave the car there until Monday morning at least. That means a lot of walking. You up for it?"

"Seems like walking's all I've been doing lately."

"Nah, you've been doing a lot of drinking too." I ducked as she threw a sofa cushion at me. "But you did sober up nicely," I added, throwing it back at her.

"Where's Dad?"

"MacGregor's. Where else?"

She wrinkled her nose. "Doesn't he *do* anything?"

"Like what?"

"I don't know," she gestured around the living room. "Like occasionally clean, or shop, or repair things here."

"Nope. Not his style."

"Do you clean?"

"Not very often," I admitted.

"So when was the last time . . ." she trailed off, tracing her finger in the dust on one of the two framed pictures in the house.

"I don't know. I do know that I usually wash my sheets every week. You'll probably want to do that soon."

"Where?"

"Laundromat down on Main Street. I try to go on Sunday mornings 'cause there's not much of a crowd. You can come with me when I go, just make sure you have a lot of quarters with you."

"Fun."

"Yep." I finished loading the snacks and sodas into my backpack. "Need anything else?"

"Don't think so."

"Let's go!"

We went out to the shed. I had been afraid to go out there, although I didn't tell Kayla that. I was afraid that the primer wouldn't be set yet, or that I would find bubbles or dirt in it. I was lucky. Everything was perfect.

Quickly we ripped the window coverings off. Being very careful not to bump the car at all, I put the compressor into the hatchback. I tossed the last of the tape and the newspaper in with it. While I opened the main doors to the shed, Kayla tossed our clothes in the back seat, and then we climbed in.

She put her seat belt on, and I started the engine. "Don't you buckle up?"

"Can't." I turned around and backed out carefully. I hopped out and quickly shut the shed doors, locking them from the inside, then went out the side door, locking it behind me.

"*Now* you can put it on," she said as I climbed back in.

"Nope. It's one of three parts that still need to be found."

"What're the other parts?"

I tapped the inside of my door. "Paneling here and the dashboard."

"Oh," she said, looking at the naked metal door next to her. Then she asked, "How does a seat belt break? Doesn't that defeat the purpose?"

"It didn't just pop out or anything," I said. "I took it out."

"Why?"

"The blood stains wouldn't come out."

"Blood stains?"

I nodded. "I get all the parts from the salvage yard. Most cars only end up there after an accident."

"Oh," she said again, more quietly.

I shifted into first, and then into second.

"I thought this was an automatic."

"It is. But you have to shift from first to second."

"Why?"

I shrugged. "Because the engineers at Honda decided to be different."

"I've never heard of an automatic that you had to shift."

"Not many people have. I had a hard time getting a healthy transmission for this one. Most of them come in burned out 'cause people didn't shift."

"I'm not surprised."

I glanced at her. "You're not old enough to drive. Why do you pay attention?"

"I used to take Mom's car out every once in a while."

"Really? How often did you get caught?"

"By the cops, never."

"By Mom?"

"Nope."

"So who caught you?"

"A neighbor, once."

"What'd they do?"

"Thanked me for driving."

"You're kidding!"

She shrugged.

I thought for a moment, then said, "Were you driving Mom?"

"Maybe."

"Was she drunk?"

"Yep."

"Mom drank. How come you never did before you got here?"

"Never had the chance. Mom kept me under her thumb and the liquor locked up."

"Oh."

We didn't really talk on the rest of way over to Jason's. I had a lot of things I wanted to think about and then ask Kayla, but right now I needed to concentrate on my driving. I couldn't afford to get pulled over. The car wasn't registered and I didn't have insurance yet. When we got to Jason's street, a lot of the tension left me.

I pulled up in front of the garage door, and started to get out.

"I can get it," she said, releasing her seat belt.

"It's locked," I said.

I went and unlocked and opened the door, then came back and pulled the car in carefully. Jason had a two-car garage, and he kept it almost spotless. I pulled in dead center. We'd have plenty of room to maneuver while painting.

Kayla was laughing and shaking her head.

"What?"

"You and Jason. You lock *everything* up, don't you?"

"Pretty much. Why?"

"Neither of you have that much to begin with. Do you really think people would try to rip you off?"

I stopped for a minute to consider what she was saying. "I think it's because we don't have much that we lock it up. Everything we have is important to us, in one way or another."

"I guess," she said, sighing as she got out of the car.

"Shut the door, will ya?" I asked. I ignored her giggle as I unlocked the interior door to the house and went into Jason's kitchen. I set the backpack of snacks on the counter, and read Jason's note.

> Stet—
> Help yourself to any food in the fridge or cabinets. I'll be back Monday, probably afternoon. Drop by the yard after school. Might have some more work for you.
> Jason
>
> P.S.—My compressor's up and running. Go ahead and use it.

"Thanks, man," I murmured, smiling. Now Kayla would be able to help me paint. "Hope you're feeling better," I added.

I opened the fridge and stared. Jason must have thought

I was bringing a whole party over. It was loaded with sodas and dip and something that looked like lasagna. There wasn't much room for the food we had brought. I left our sodas in the backpack.

When I got back out to the garage, Kayla had already started taping the windows.

"Hey!"

"What?" she stopped instantly and peered at me. "Am I doing it wrong? Do you tape them differently this time?"

"No, you're doing it right. Keep up the good work."

"Then what's wrong?"

"Nothing," I said. "Everything's just better than I thought it would be. I'm not used to it."

Kayla gave me one last funny look and went back to the windows. I began sorting through the cans of paint. Jason had even left several empty buckets for mixing, and a few old sheets to use as dropcloths.

It took us a good thirty minutes to get everything set up. Finally the windows were all taped, the dropcloths were down, both compressors were primed, and the sketchbook was spread open on the workbench.

"Now what?" she asked when I paused.

"Now," I said, pulling out a box of chalk. "The work actually begins." I handed her a piece of chalk. "We need to outline first. We're not going to do any of the little details. Those will have to be freehand. But the main lines, especially the wings, we want to make sure will be even on both sides. We'll start together on the hood, then work our way to the back."

"Are you sure you shouldn't be the one to do this?" she asked me doubtfully.

"I thought you were here to help."

"Well, I am, but—"

"Well, then, help!" I said, grinning at her.

The outlining took us almost another full hour. We kept walking back and forth, comparing our lines, making sure we were even. We almost never were, so then we had to decide which line looked better. It took all of our time and concentration.

"Now what?" Kayla asked again when we finally finished.

"Now, we put a brown base coat inside the chalk lines."

"Shouldn't we do the top first?"

I looked at her. She squirmed a little. "So the paint don't run down into the falcon later?" I just stared at her. "Okay, okay, you know what you're doing."

"Actually, I don't think I do," I said. "You're right. We should do the blue first. Thanks. I knew you were good for somethin'."

She blushed.

"Need to take a break before we get started? 'Cause we can't stop till the first coat's done," I warned.

"I'm doin' all right."

"Let's get started then. Ever work an airbrush?"

"No." She shook her head, wide-eyed.

"Crash course," I said, turning toward the compressors.

"Maybe I should just watch," she said, taking a step back.

"You said you were gonna help," I said, grabbing her hand. "Now come on."

"Stet, I don't want to wreck your car!"

"Don't worry, I won't let you."

I picked up the nozzle and pointed it toward the wall. "You need to keep your arm the same distance from the car the whole time, and you need to move the same speed. If you get closer or you go slower, the paint will be darker." I started spraying the wall. "See?"

Kayla nodded. I handed her the nozzle. "Your turn."

"Won't Jason be mad that we're painting his wall?"

"It's just water," I said. "And if for some reason it does stain the wall, I'll repaint his garage."

I watched her for a few minutes, but it didn't take long for her to get the hang of it. She had a steady hand and a natural gift. I told her so and she laughed.

"I just hope I can do it when I'm painting your car."

"You will," I said. I went over and opened a can of blue paint. "I'll get the compressor ready for you."

"Suddenly I need to go to the bathroom," she said. "I'll be right back."

I had both compressors loaded when she got back. She was carrying two sodas and a bag of chips.

"Just in case," she said with a grin.

I handed her the nozzle. "Just relax," I said. "You'll do fine."

"Do we need bandanas again?"

I winced. "I forgot them. Sorry."

She gave me the nozzle back and ran over to her bag. A few seconds later, she had two bandanas in hand, one purple, one pink. "Which would you prefer?" she asked, grinning.

"I think the purple one's more my color," I said dryly.

After she had tied her bandana on, I said, "Now are we ready?" She nodded, but her eyes glittered uncertainly over the pink fabric. "Just remember to stay above the chalk line, okay?"

She nodded again, took the nozzle from me, and got started. I immediately turned and started with my compressor. I didn't want to make her nervous by watching, and if she was doing it wrong, I'd just have to go back and fix it later anyway.

After a few minutes of working in the hums of the compressors, I asked, "Did Mom drink a lot?"

"What?" Kayla looked at me.

"Did Mom get drunk a lot?" I asked again, louder.

"Well, I thought she did, but then I moved here. She didn't drink as much as Dad does."

"But you think she was an alcoholic?"

"Yeah."

"Dad is too."

"I know."

"You know that they say alcoholism is hereditary?"

"Yeah." We were quiet again, then she said, "So that's why you don't drink, right?"

"Kind of."

"You've said that before. Come on, tell me."

"I was young and stupid."

"Oh? And you're old and wise now?"

I laughed. "Okay, so I was younger and stupider. Is that better?"

"Much."

"My friends and I started drinking when I was in eighth grade. We drank a lot. It was easy and no one really cared. We'd take a six-pack from Dad one day, from somebody else's folks the next."

"How many of you were there?"

"Five or seven of us, depending on the day."

"So you weren't drinking heavily."

"Well . . ."

"What?"

"We'd also take bottles of liquor when we could."

"Still, it doesn't sound like that big of a deal."

Behind my bandana, I smiled. "That's what we thought too."

"Until?"

"We thought it was boring to just sit around someone's house and drink. We wanted more action. So we started taking joyrides."

I paused, but Kayla didn't say anything. She appeared focused on the painting.

"We never went very far. Hell, we were only thirteen and didn't really have anywhere to go. So we just screwed around. I can't even remember what we were doing the day we wrecked, but I know we were punching each other in the back of the car."

Just thinking about it made me start shaking. I turned off the compressor to finish the story. I hadn't told anyone about it, ever—not even Jason—and I hadn't thought about it in a long time. But once I started, I couldn't stop.

"We ran into a trailer. And I'm really glad we did. None of us were hurt. Neither were the two people in the truck pulling the trailer. But the horses . . ."

Kayla's eyes suddenly flashed up to my face.

"They had to shoot one of them right there. Both the back legs were busted, and it was screaming—God, what an awful sound! A bellow that just rips your heart out. They tried to get the other one to calm down. It was pretty hurt too. They got it to the vet, but I guess there was too much damage. They had to put it down."

"How horrible!"

"Yeah, it really was. And what's worse, is all I could think was 'Thank God they're only *horses*.' I mean, how would I feel if they had been *people* we had killed?"

"Were you the one driving?"

"No," I said, shaking my head. I took a deep breath and turned the compressor back on. "That was Tony," I added as I began painting again.

"Tony? With brown wavy hair and green eyes?"

"That's him."

"But he still drives! How'd he get his license?"

"Just because he drives doesn't mean he has a license." Then I looked at her. "How'd you know about Tony?"

"He's one of the guys I met at MacGregor's."

I had to shut the compressor off again.

"What?"

"He's one of—"

"Is he the one you left with the other night?"

"Yeah."

I swore. "Kayla, you really know how to pick them, don't you?"

Her troubled eyes looked at me over the bandana. "Don't tell me he has a girlfriend too!"

"He doesn't," I said. Relief showed in her eyes before I added, "He's got a wife."

"What?" she squealed as she turned off her compressor. "What do you mean, he has a wife?"

"I mean he got married last summer."

"But he's your age!"

"So? Most of the guys I grew up with are married now, and have a kid too."

"Tony has a kid?"

"Cute little girl. Just a couple months old," I said. I sighed and turned my compressor back on, shaking my head as I did so.

"I didn't know!" Kayla wailed. "I swear, Stet, he never told me!"

"Was he wearing his ring?"

"I didn't look! It never crossed my mind that he might be married!"

"Doesn't matter. I doubt he had it on anyway." I almost started to berate her for being stupid, then I remembered that she was only fourteen. I wouldn't have thought about anyone being married at that age either. "Come on," I said. "Let's finish the sky." She turned her compressor on, and we finished the roof and top of the hatchback.

I showed her how to clean out the nozzles, and we reloaded with a gold-brown mix for the base coat.

As we got started, Kayla said, "The sooner I get out of here, the better. All I'm doin' is screwin' up."

"That ain't true," I said. "You've just had a rough week. All things considered, I think you're doin' pretty good."

"You can't be serious."

"Yeah, I am. I mean, you just lost your Mom, and you get shipped off to here, which ain't exactly paradise. You discover you've got a drunk for a father, and that your brother's just some salvage yard trash who's hangin' on to his high school career with the last bit of his fingernails.

Then you get pukin' drunk. But you're still tryin' to get by and you haven't freaked out. You're doin' pretty good."

Kayla's eyes had been getting bigger as I had gone on, and now she just started laughing. "Thanks. Why do I feel so much worse now?"

I grinned behind my bandana. "'Cause I'm just a confidence-inspirin' kind of guy."

She shook her head and focused on the painting again.

"You still think you're gonna leave?" I asked after a few minutes.

Shrugging, she said, "I don't know. I'm tryin' to."

"Where're you gonna, go?"

"I sent my—our—cousin another letter. The one I told you about?"

"The one in Kansas?"

"Yep. Sent it the first day I was here. She probably got it two days after the first one, but I was feeling a little desperate."

"And you still want to go."

"Not much has improved," she said. "I really don't see a reason to stay."

I nodded, and kept my eyes on the car. I didn't want her to see that what she said hurt.

After a few long seconds, she said, "Stet?"

"Yeah?"

She didn't say anything right away, so I looked up. She was watching me. "Why don't you come too?"

"What, and leave all this?" I shook my head. "No thanks."

"Seriously. Why don't you? There's nothing for you here."

"I'm close to graduation."

"So? You could graduate from another school. Just transfer."

I shook my head again. "I know what's going on here. I can make it."

"But why stay here if you don't have to?"

"It's okay, Kayla," I said. "This is how I've lived all my life. I don't know any other way." It was true. All the times I thought about running away, what kept me here was safety. I might not have had a glamorous or easy life, but I knew how to deal with everything.

"Well, I haven't heard back yet. For all I know, Mom's cousin may not want me anyway. But will you at least think about it?"

"Kayla—"

"Please?"

"Okay, okay. I'll think about it" But I already had.

We finished the base for the falcon and cleaned out the nozzles. Then I stopped for a minute to study Kayla's drawing. She opened the bag of chips and began inhaling them.

"Hungry?"

As she put more chips in her mouth, she nodded.

"You can stop and eat if you want."

"What about you?"

"Not really hungry."

"You should eat something."

"Maybe later." I tapped the drawing. "I'd like to do the hood, if that's okay. You want to do the wings?"

"I want to help, but I think you should do the rest. I don't want to screw any of it up."

"You're a good artist," I said. "You'll do fine."

"I can draw," she agreed, "but I can't paint. I think I'll leave it to you, if that's okay."

"You'll get bored."

She shrugged. "I'm sure I can find something. Jason's got TV, right?"

I laughed. "Yeah. He don't have much, but he's got a TV."

"Well, I'm gonna go fix that pasta-salad-in-a-box that we brought. And I expect you to eat some!" She added as she went into the house.

I picked up my compressor and went to work. She came in later with some food for me, but I barely saw her. I was coaxing the falcon to life.

From time to time I had to stop to reload or change paints, but the night got away from me. Kayla came in and out a few times, staying for a while and then going back in for something.

As I watched the paint change the salvage yard car into a cruising machine, I felt like I could fly away on the falcon's wings, grab life with its talons, and see the world with its piercing eyes. By the time I finally stopped, dawn's gray sky was outside, but the Falcon had emerged from the car, full of spirit and fire.

● ● ●

When Jason's alarm sounded four hours later, it took me several seconds to find it and shut it off. I got off his still-made bed, and went to the bathroom first. Then I went to the living room. Kayla had been sleeping on the couch when I finally came in.

She wasn't there now. The door to the garage was open

a crack. I went out, and had to grin. I had been afraid I had only dreamed how good the Falcon looked, but it was real.

"Stet," Kayla murmured from the other side of the car, "this is amazing."

"You did a good job," I said.

"I didn't do anything! You're the one who made this from scratch."

"It was your design."

"You painted it," she retorted.

"Okay. We work well together as a team, how's that?"

"Cool," she said, smiling.

Almost against my will, I walked around the car, slowly. There was no sign of bubbles, dirt, or drips. It looked nearly perfect.

"*Nearly* perfect?" Kayla asked, making me jump. I didn't know I had said it out loud. "It *is* perfect! There's nothin' wrong at all!"

I opened my mouth, but then changed my mind and just smiled instead. I could have pointed out where one wing rose a little higher than the other, or that one highlight on the eyeball was slightly off, or where a few of the feathers were missing some white, but I didn't. It was nearly perfect and that was fine with me.

"Come on," I said, forcing myself to move away. "Time to get going."

"Already?"

"Yeah. If I want to open the yard on time, we got to get goin' now."

"Okay," she said quickly. "Let me grab the box of cereal. We can munch on the way."

My stomach suddenly growled. It was very loud in the garage. "Sounds good," I said, blushing because she had turned so quickly to stare at me.

"I told you to eat last night," she said, disappearing into the house.

I took one last look at my car, the Falcon, turned off the light, and then followed her.

CHAPTER FOURTEEN

IT WAS slow all day. I think we had six people come in from noon to four, and only two of them bought anything. In spite of the slowness, Kayla stayed.

We played a lot of cards, and told each other some more stories about growing up.

"Hey, do you think we could make cookies this weekend?"

"Cookies? What brings this up?" I asked, scooping up a trick.

"When I was little, I usually played out in the backyard. Sometimes she'd bake a batch of cookies and then bring the beaters out to me, when I wasn't expecting it." She smiled softly. "It was really cool."

"I bet."

She picked up the next trick and said, "Did Dad ever do anything cool like that for you?"

"He took me for a pony ride a couple of times. Wanted me to be a rider like him."

"I just can't imagine him as a cowboy."

"You saw the trophies. His specialty was bronc riding. But he apparently hadn't thought about the risks until he took me."

"What do you mean?"

"The pony gave a little buck and threw me off. I thought Dad was going to kill it with his bare hands." I tossed down my card and shook my head. "It was the last time he ever took me riding."

Kayla's eyes were wide. "How sweet!"

"What?"

"He was that worried about you getting hurt! Mom never worried like that."

"She probably did but you just don't remember it."

"Maybe," she said.

She napped for a little while on the cot in the back, and I finished repairing a blender a lady had brought in. At quarter till four, Kayla asked how long we had to stay.

"Getting bored?"

"A little. But I know I want to eat dinner tonight. If you have to stay, then I'll go pick something up."

"How do you stay so skinny? All you ever do is eat!"

"Well, it's obvious that you're skinny 'cause you *never* eat. And that's worse."

"I do too eat!"

"Not very often."

I shrugged that away.

"So when do you close today?"

"About ten minutes."

"Really?"

"Yep."

"Cool!" After a few seconds, she said, "Then what are we gonna do?"

I laughed. "You're always asking that."

"I like to know what's goin' on. So what's goin' on?"

"I don't know. What do you want to do? I've been making all the other decisions."

"That's because I don't know what there is to do around here."

"What do you usually do?"

"Back home?"

"Yeah."

She frowned in thought. "We'd go hang out at the arcade—"

"I thought you said that was for junior high kids," I interrupted.

She blushed. "We *used* to go out to the arcade, when we were in junior high," she said defensively.

I almost pointed out that she was in junior high last year, but I didn't. "Okay, so what do the big cool high schoolers do?"

She ignored my sarcasm. "Oh, hang out at the mall mostly. Sometimes go skating."

"Skateboarding?"

"No, no. Ice-skating. We had a rink close by. Could skate for three hours for two bucks."

"Well, we don't have that stuff around here. The mall's about twenty miles away, and the closest thing to a skating rink is a little pond behind the café, and I'm pretty sure it's not frozen over yet."

"So what are we gonna do?"

I spread my hands out. "I don't know."

"What do you usually do?"

"Work on the car."

"And that's pretty much done." Her smile lit up her whole being. "That's gotta feel really good."

"Yeah," I said, and I knew I was grinning back. "It does."

"So what are you gonna do now?"

"I think I might hit you the next time you ask that!"

She knew I was joking and laughed. "I mean, you're not gonna have that anymore, so how are you gonna fill those empty hours?"

"Cruisin' in the car, of course."

"Could we do that now?" Kayla sounded really excited.

I shook my head. "Paint's gotta dry."

"I knew that," she said, disgusted with herself.

"I do want to stay at Jason's tonight, so I can get the car out of his garage before he gets home tomorrow."

"It's okay to say you want to drive it as soon as you can."

"Well, that too."

"We should go celebrate. Want to go to MacGregor's?"

I hesitated. I really didn't want to go, but the only other choices were the café and two fast-food joints. MacGregor's made a good chicken-fried steak, had pool tables, a small dance floor. Kayla was looking at me with hopeful eyes and—"Yeah. Let's go to MacGregor's."

● ● ●

Three times walking to MacGregor's I almost suggested we go someplace else. And when we got to the door, I stopped. Although I couldn't see through the door, I could hear the muffled music.

"Stet?" Kayla looked at me. "You okay?"

I had my hand on the handle, but I wasn't sure I could move. People I knew would be in there, people I had avoided for a long enough time to make it awkward. I had never done any of my drinking at MacGregor's, but the thought of picking up another drink terrified me. And I wasn't sure I'd be able to refuse one if it was offered.

"Stet?" Now Kayla looked nervous.

"I'm fine," I said, giving myself a little shake and pulling the door open. The honky-tonk music blew past us, mingled with cigarette smoke. "Ladies first," I said, giving a little bow. She smiled and walked in. I only wished I felt part of the confidence she was showing.

In old TV movies, everything stops when the right or wrong person walks into the bar. It wasn't quite that bad, but it was close. The music was from a jukebox, so it kept going. There were several people who glanced up but just returned to what they were doing, and there were several more that didn't look at all. Then there were the people who did stop and stare. My father and Tony were two of them.

Dad pushed himself away from the bar, leaning a little too far to one side. He grinned, then motioned with the hand holding his beer to an empty table close by, spilling much of the beer on the floor. The old joke about spilling your drink being alcohol abuse flew through my mind, but it only made me sad.

Kayla looked back at me, and I shrugged. She went to the table he indicated, and I followed.

"Well I'll be damned," Dad said, as we sat down. "I never thought I'd see the day you were willing to grace us with your presence."

I shrugged again as I pulled out the laminated menu cards stuck between the salt and pepper shakers.

"It always amazed me that you spent all day working with scraps and garbage but considered yourself better than the rest of us."

"What's the score, Dad?" Kayla asked, pointing toward

the TV. He turned around to see the screen. I handed her one of the menus.

"Don't know. Haven't really been watching." He continued to watch for a few minutes while Kayla scanned the menu. I looked around.

Tony and Chris were shooting pool. When Chris looked over, he smiled and nodded at me and I nodded back. Then he turned to Tony and said something that made them both laugh. Chuck was putting some more money in the jukebox, and a few other guys I had gone to school with were at the bar.

"What are you having?" Kayla asked me.

"Chicken-fried steak."

"Huh?" she asked, leaning forward to hear better. I tapped her menu instead. "Is it good?" I gave her a thumbs-up.

Dad turned back around. "Game's over," he said to Kayla. "Someone must've won." He looked at me. "So what really brought you here?"

"He finished the car last night," Kayla said brightly.

Dad gave her a startled glance, then looked back at me. "Is that true?"

I nodded, keeping my mouth tightly closed and wishing Kayla had done the same.

"About damn time," he said.

"What can I get for ya?" a bleached blonde waitress asked us, tapping her pad of paper with her pen.

"Two chicken-fried steaks," Kayla said, pointing at the menu.

"That all?"

"Yep," she said.

The waitress started to turn away. "A pitcher of beer here," Dad said.

I felt my mouth go dry. The waitress turned back. "How many glasses?"

"Three," he snapped. "Can't you count?"

Kayla shook her head. "Just one glass for him," she said. "But we'd also like a couple of sodas."

The waitress nodded curtly and left.

"What? You too good to drink with your old man all of a sudden?"

"No," she said, shaking her head. "I just need something to eat first."

Dad shook his head; clearly that didn't make any sense to him. But he didn't say anything else about it. Instead, he turned back for me.

"So the car's done. That mean you're gonna get a life now?"

"I've got a life, thanks."

"You're gonna have to get a job to pay for insurance. I ain't payin' it for ya."

"Didn't ask you to."

"You could get a good full-time job at the mill. We need more people. First time in twenty years we actually need more men."

"Not till I'm done with school."

"Stet, a diploma don't mean that much."

"It does to me."

"It ain't gonna affect your pay."

I stared at the dance floor, watching a few people dance.

Dad sighed and turned back to Kayla. "You better be at school tomorrow mornin'. I'm goin' to the mill early and then I'll meet you there at eight. And it better not take more then thirty minutes, 'cause that's all I've got. The boss is pissed I'm takin' that much time anyway."

Kayla nodded.

We sat in silence until our order came. Dad was drinking his beer and Kayla and I were watching people.

The waitress set down the pitcher, two sodas, and three glasses. "This way if y'all change your minds, I don't have to come back," she said. She set down the two dinner platters, both of them dripping gravy on the table. "Anything else?" she asked as she set the bill down and walked away.

Kayla looked at me. "Guess not," she said. I smiled.

We started eating. Dad poured himself a full glass of beer, and then poured two more and set them in front of us.

"A toast," he said, holding up his glass.

Kayla picked up her beer. Trying to finish my bite, I picked up my soda. Dad rolled his eyes.

"To finishing Stetson's car," Dad began, and for a brief moment I was almost touched. "Probably the only thing he'll ever complete," he finished, and took a big swallow of beer. I just put my glass back down. Kayla looked at me in confusion. Shrugging and shaking my head, I went back to my dinner.

"Well," Dad said, belching, "I hate to leave this exciting family dinner, but you two are just dull." He stood up with his glass in one hand and the pitcher in the other. "I don't think you'll miss this," he said, and he wandered back to the bar.

Kayla leaned forward. "What was that all about?"

"Nothing,'" I said, shaking my head. There was no point

in my trying to explain what I barely understood myself. It had taken me nearly ten years to realize that my father was jealous of success. What I still didn't know was if it was anyone's success or mine in particular that set him off.

"Well, at least we can try to enjoy the rest of our meal," she said.

"And pay for his beer."

She stared at me for a moment, then snatched up the bill. Almost immediately she started to get up.

I reached out and put a hand on her arm. "Just sit down and eat," I said.

"But he— You didn't— We—" Kayla spluttered.

"It don't matter," I said. I kept my eyes on her face and didn't let go of her arm until she nodded and picked up her fork.

"I think you should leave town with me," she said a few minutes later.

Before I could reply, Tony appeared at our table.

"Hey, Stet, how're ya doin'?"

"Fine," I said, finishing my soda.

"Kayla, you look better every time you come in here," he said, staring at her tight-fitting T-shirt.

"How's Vicky doin'?" I asked mildly.

Tony shot me an angry look, but answered just as mildly, "Fine. She says hi."

I nodded, but he had already turned back to Kayla.

"I think you owe me a dance." He smiled. Tony always got the girls when he smiled.

She shook her head.

"The other night you said you'd dance with me. We never got the chance."

"I don't feel like dancing," Kayla said.

"Come on," Tony said, picking up her hand and pulling. "Let's go."

I could tell Kayla was trying to get her hand back. "No!"

"Tony," I began, but I'd like to think he didn't hear me.

"You owe me!" He said. Somehow his smile wasn't quite the same. He pulled Kayla out of her chair.

I stood up as he tried to pass me. We had always been the same height but I had rarely been able to stare down his green eyes. Tonight I could.

"Be back in a little bit, Stet," he said.

"She doesn't want to go."

"Aw, she's just saying that. They always want to go."

"No, I don't!" Kayla said, tying to break his grip.

Tony started to go around me, and I stepped right into him. "Let her go."

"What?"

"You heard me."

Suddenly Kayla broke free of him and took a few steps back, rubbing her wrist. I knew that everyone in the bar must be watching, but I didn't care.

"Leave her alone," I said.

"Hey, man, I let her go."

"Leave her alone," I repeated. "If you touch her again, I'll kill you."

Tony laughed, inches from my face. "You couldn't even draw blood."

"Make the first move."

"Stet," Kayla said. "Let's just go, okay?"

Tony moved forward the last possible inch before we

started touching. "What kind of move would you like?"

"Any kind. It's time somebody shut you up."

"He don't mean that, Tony," Dad said, pulling me away from him. I hadn't realized he was right behind me.

"Yes, I did."

"Stet, why don't you go cool down somewhere else?"

I shook off my father's hand and pulled my chair around to sit down. Dad's hand came down on top of mine. "I really think you ought to leave," he said in a low voice.

Kayla came around to my side of the table. "Come on, Stet. Let's get out of here."

Other than the Randy Travis song coming from the jukebox, it was quiet. No one was talking. The mill workers were all looking at us, and several of them were standing by their chairs. Kayla gave my shoulder a push, and we walked quickly out of the bar. As I pushed the front door open, I heard my father say, "Come on, Tony, I'll buy you a beer."

I almost turned back around. How dare he! How dare he support Tony instead of me, instead of Kayla!

"Stet?" Kayla sounded worried, and I realized that I was making a weird growl in the back of my throat.

I shoved the door open so hard and so fast that it slammed against the outside wall, and the glass cracked. Quickly I strode across the parking lot. Kayla was almost jogging just to keep up with me.

By the time we had gotten to the café, I had a stitch in my side. I slowed down.

"Thank you."

I glanced at her. "Sorry. Didn't mean to go so fast."

"No, I meant thank you for back there. No one's ever stood up for me before."

I smiled at her. "Thank you too. I've never had any one stand up for me, either."

"I didn't—"

"You told Dad. You were almost bragging about me."

"Well, I think it's pretty cool, and—"

"I know you do. Thank you."

"You're welcome," she said. "Are we going to Jason's now?"

"Unless you want to do something else."

"No. I want to go see your cool car."

"With your cool design."

Each step away from MacGregor's felt better than the one before.

CHAPTER FIFTEEN

"WELL? WHAT are you waiting for?"

The garage door was open. Kayla was sitting in the passenger seat, and I was behind the wheel. The key was in the ignition. But I didn't turn it.

From the front seats, you couldn't see the Falcon's eyes or open beak; you couldn't see the wings that wrapped almost protectively around the side of the car, encasing those inside. If you ignored the missing side panels, the cracked brown dashboard, and the missing driver's seat belt, you'd never know this car had been put together nearly piece by piece, that for two years all that held it together were hours of hard work, sweat, and love.

"Stet, I really don't want to be late."

I nodded and put my hand on the key again. But I still didn't turn it.

The car would draw a lot of attention, but the people who saw it wouldn't see the dream that had come true, the only goal I truly believed I could reach. Now that I was there, I didn't know what to do next.

"Would you like me to drive?" she asked sweetly.

I rolled my eyes at her.

"So what's wrong?"

"I don't know. Just a feeling."

"A feeling?"

"Yeah. It feels like it's all over."

She looked at me strangely. "You're kiddin', right?"

"No."

"Building it's over, yeah. But cruisin' in it is just beginning. And the places it's gonna take you—places you've never dreamed of.

"How do you know?"

She smiled. "Just a feeling."

I smiled back.

"Now can we go?"

In answer, I turned the key, and under the Falcon the engine began to purr. My smile got bigger. "Sweetest sound."

"If you say so," she said. "I'd like to hear the wind blowing, so I'd know we're moving."

"If I'm not going fast enough for you," I said, putting the Falcon into reverse, "feel free to get out and walk."

I backed slowly out of the garage.

"If this is as fast as you're gonna go, I may have to walk."

"Why don't you walk up to the garage and shut the door?" I asked.

She stuck her tongue out at me, undid her seat belt, and got out of the car. I pulled the Falcon out into the street and then waited for her. Before she had even shut the door, we were moving.

"Give me a second!"

"Thought I was moving too slow!"

"Well, yeah, but that doesn't mean you have to throw me out of the car!"

I did my best to stay off Main Street on the way to school. It's a favorite place for the cops to hang out, and my car would be sure to be noticed. First the sheriff would notice the paint job, and then, as he continued to stare, he would notice the lack of plates. Although heads turned on every street, none of them belonged to a cop.

As we pulled into the school parking lot, Kayla said, "I think you just gave yourself thirty new wrinkles. Why don't you smile and enjoy this?"

I started to pull into the parking lot, but then kept going.

"What are you doing?"

"Can't park in front," I said. "Car's not registered or anything. You religious?"

"Why?"

"Pray that I don't get a ticket today, okay?"

She smiled and I felt a little better.

Even though I went around the corner, off school property, it seemed like we were instantly mobbed. People I barely knew, some I didn't even recognize, were standing around, asking questions, reaching out to trace along a feather.

"Awesome!"

"Where'd you get it done?"

"How much did it cost?"

"Whoa! That's tight!"

"You got a name for this bird?"

At that I looked for Kayla. "Do we have a name for it?"

She shrugged. "It's your bird now," she said. "I think I just saw Dad go in. I better get goin'. Meet here after school?"

"Yeah." I looked around, uncertain as to what to do. I didn't want to stay here with all these people who suddenly wanted to talk to me, but I didn't feel comfortable leaving my car with them, either. I answered a few of the questions being shouted at me.

"Yeah, I painted it. . . . That was Kayla, my sister. . . . She came up with the design. I rebuilt the whole thing. . . . About two years . . . No, it was just me. . . . Couldn't afford a Mustang. . . ." Then I couldn't take it anymore and bolted for the building. I had never been so glad to go into school.

I pulled the door open and found myself face to face with Mr. Kincaid. He blinked in the sunlight and held his hand up to shield his eyes. "Stetson?"

"Hey." I moved to go around him.

"You know what's going on out there?" he asked, holding the door open.

"People are checkin' out my car," I said, taking a few steps inside.

"What's wrong with it?" he was still in the doorway.

I stopped and turned back to him. "Nothin'. It's finished, that's all."

"So there's no problem out there? No fight?"

Suddenly I realized that's probably what it looked like, with all the people standing in a ring around my car. "No. No problem, no fight."

He stepped back in the building and let the door close. "You got a minute?"

I hesitated, and the bell rang.

"Come on," he said, inclining his head. "Let's go talk in my office for a minute. I'll write you a pass."

"I thought I only had to come in during lunch," I muttered, falling into step with him.

"Yeah, but if we do this now, I might let you off this week. How's that sound?"

I shrugged, and I could tell it wasn't quite the enthusiastic reply he had been looking for. We went into his office and he shut the door behind me.

"First, the good news. Mrs. Dobson has agreed to let you into her class."

"I thought that was already decided."

"Mr. Johnson thought it fair to ask if she was willing to add you to her class."

"You mean he's still looking for a way to get rid of me."

Mr. Kincaid opened his mouth to say something, but then closed it and just nodded. "But you didn't hear anything from me."

"So what's the good news?"

"The good news is that you could take the GED next week and get this all over with. I've checked, and it's being offered on Wednes—"

"I thought I told you I want my diploma."

"Yeah, Stet, you did. But I'm afraid you might not realize how hard it's really going to be for you to stay here the rest of the year. You're going to be held to a higher standard, because of your record. One sneeze at the wrong time in the wrong class could get you kicked out."

"If that happens, I'll take the GED then."

"It's not offered all the time, Stet, and I really think—"

"I'll worry about it when I need to. Right now you're making me miss class when I promised I wouldn't."

Mr. Kincaid gave me a long look, then he sighed. "You're right." He pulled a pad of paper over to him. "I'll let you go."

"And I can wait till next week to come in to talk to you again?"

"Yeah," he said, handing me the pass.

I was opening the door when he said, "Stet, I want you to understand, it's not that I don't think you can make it. I just want you to be realistic."

"I'll be realistic. And you can be realistic too. I know you don't think I can make it, any more than my dad does. And I'm gonna laugh at all of you during graduation."

"I hope so, Stet. I really do."

I shook my head but didn't say the words that came to mind. Instead I just walked out the door.

● ● ●

The rest of the day was interesting. Everyone was talking about my car, and I used it as a chance to talk up my shirts. I spent lunchtime at a cafeteria table discussing shirts and airbrushing with a group of people I hardly knew.

I kept looking for Kayla in the halls, but I never saw her, not even at lunch. I figured that she must have almost the opposite of my schedule.

Unfortunately, I did pass Ms. Pepper in the hallway, and she almost scared me. She didn't look through me or give me a false little smile. She glared at me for a full five seconds, and I swear she bared her teeth at me as she went by.

By the end of the day, I was exhausted. My emotions were too tightly strung. I was worried about the condition of my car, about Jason, about how Kayla was doing, and about how I was going to work at the yard this week and still get those shirts done.

Somehow I had promised to do ten shirts, and had six or seven more people who were going to bring in pictures or designs for me to look at. I had also agreed to look at a couple of cars. The idea of airbrushing someone else's car was a little intimidating, but I could make a lot more money doing that than doing one shirt at a time.

I didn't want to go to my locker after school, so I actually took a textbook out the door with me. After carefully walking around my car, I took a sigh of relief. No one had touched her. I put my book in the back seat, hoping I would remember it the next morning, and then waited for Kayla.

And waited.

Fifteen minutes after the last bell rang, the parking lot was nearly empty, and Kayla still wasn't there.

I didn't know what to do. Should I leave her? Wait a little longer? Go look for her?

I paced around the Falcon for a few more moments. I was going to be late for work. I got in, put the key in the ignition, pulled it back out, and got out again. I started walking back into school, but then I stopped again.

The front door opened, and I expected to see Kayla coming out. Instead, I saw Chip and Julie. They were arguing about something and didn't see me until they were only a few feet away.

Julie ignored me as usual. Chip gave me a distracted smile and said, "Hey, man." They both kept walking.

"Did you see Kayla today?"

"Who?"

"My sister." At his blank look, I added, "The one you took out to lunch last week?"

Julie came to an abrupt halt. "What?" she practically spat.

Chip looked at her and then back at me. "Don't know

what you're talking about, man," he put his arm around Julie and started walking.

I sighed. "She's about this tall," I said, holding my hand to my shoulder, "has dark hair, was wearing a miniskirt today."

They kept walking. Julie was saying something to Chip and he was shaking his head.

I opened my mouth to call him some choice words when I heard, "Stetson. How was your first day back?"

I turned to face Mr. Johnson's blindingly false smile. "Fine."

"No trouble?"

"No."

"Funny, I thought I saw your name on the attendance list."

"What?"

"For missing your afternoon classes."

I spread my hands out. "I'm still here. Been here since seven." Around a growing bad taste in my mouth, I asked, "Was it my sister's name?"

Mr. Johnson's eyebrows rose. "Hadn't thought about that. Yes, I suppose it could have been. Ahem. Well, then, Stetson, I'm glad your first day on contract was successful. Let's keep the rest of the year like that." And he turned on his heel and left.

My teeth were clenched and I could feel the tension throughout my body. For the second time in two days, I was ready to get violent because of Kayla.

Instead, I went back to the Falcon, climbed in, and drove away. I never looked back at school. If Kayla came out now, she could just walk home.

As I drove to the salvage yard, I was seething. The problem was that I didn't know who I was mad at—Kayla or myself. Kayla hadn't been there, but I had let myself trust her.

The bright spot of my day was finding the gates to the salvage yard open and Jason's car parked alongside the office. I pulled the Falcon up so it was directly in front of the open office door.

Jason came glowering to the door, but at least he was wearing a tie-dye patch. "Stet—" He started to yell, but then his jaw dropped, literally.

"Close your trap," I said with a grin as I got out. "You'll catch flies or something."

He closed it, and he began to beam. "You got 'er done. She's gorgeous!"

"You don't have to sound so surprised," I said.

"I knew you were good, but—Stet, you could sell this and make a small fortune!" He began to walk around the car slowly, inspecting it carefully.

"No way, man. This is my life right here."

"You could probably name your price and then buy two more cars to fix up."

I shook my head firmly.

Jason shrugged. "Do it your way."

"What else is new?"

"Not much," he said, having completed the walk around the Falcon. "Looks like you did good this weekend. Finished the car and made us some money here."

"Yeah," I said, fishing the register and office keys out of my pocket. I held them out to him, but he waved them away.

"Keep 'em. I'm sure you'll need 'em again."

"What'd the doc say?" I asked, following him into the office.

"Nothin' good," he said. He walked around behind the counter and sat down on the stool.

"What's that mean?"

"Don't know."

"Jason," I said, feeling my frustration wash back over me. "You said we'd talk."

"I know. We will. But I need to decide what I'm gonna do before I talk about it"

"About what?"

"I got a choice to make," he said, pulling the record books closer to him. "And it's very personal."

"Jason—"

"Stet." If Jason had been mad, I would have blown up right then. But he just sounded tired. So tired. "When I'm ready, you'll be the first to know. Did you get all the cars stripped?"

"Working on the last one," I said, accepting the change in conversation.

"Go ahead and get it done tonight if you can. I got three more comin' in tomorrow mornin'."

"Okay," I said, turning toward the door.

"Hey, where's that sister of yours?"

"Don't know," I said, walking out. "Don't care."

● ● ●

It didn't take me long to finish stripping the last car. I stocked the parts and headed back to the office with the toolbox. Goosebumps stood out on my arms. I was gonna have to start wearing my jacket soon.

As I came around the corner, Jason was getting out of my car. He saw me, appeared startled, and shoved a piece of paper into his pocket.

"Hey," I said. "What's up?"

"Just checkin' your interior work. You put it together real good." He looked guilty.

"Thanks."

"What're you gonna do to the dash?"

"Think I may have to use your idea and cover it with the last of the carpet."

He nodded and shifted from one foot to the other. "Done strippin' the car?" he asked abruptly.

"Yeah."

"Good. Good."

We stood there in awkward silence. Jason cleared his throat. "Now's the time to clean out the office."

I groaned. "Do I have to?" Cleaning out the office was a week-long project when I was working full-time. Dusting and wiping things down could take a full day, and then I'd have to sort through the various piles and decide what to reshelve or throw away.

"No," Jason said, taking me by surprise.

"I don't?"

"No. You could just go home, take the rest of the day off."

"But you wouldn't pay me for that."

He snorted. "Of course not!"

"Guess I'd better start cleaning then."

"Only if you want to," he said with a smile.

"Yeah, yeah, yeah." I walked toward the office door, then paused to took over my shoulder. "You gonna help or just sit and daydream in my car again?"

Without looking up from the Falcon, he absently flipped me off.

I went into the office and looked around. Then I decided that the best way to start was from the back of the room and move to the front. Unfortunately, that also meant I started with the bathroom. As I stood in the bathroom door, I decided that if I could get it clean before I left for the night, I would be doing well.

An hour and a half later, the bathroom was cleaner than it had been in months. I stretched, feeling the muscles and bones in my back pull against each other. I wasn't used to scrubbing like that.

"Hello? Anyone here?" Kayla's voice drifted back to me.

I came out of the bathroom just as she came in through the office door.

"There you are! I've been looking for you!" she said, smiling.

"Oh really?" I retorted. "Must not've been looking too hard. I've been exactly where I said I'd be."

Her smile faltered. "I tried to find you at lunch. I thought we could go out."

"Don't have the money to go out for lunch, remember?"

"I thought just this once—"

"Once? You've been eating out since you got here! Did you get a job to pay for it yet?"

"Why are you so pissed?" she asked.

"Why? Why am I pissed?"

"That's what I said!"

"Where were you after school?"

"I went . . ." she trailed off.

"You went where? Not to meet me at the car."

She closed her eyes. "I'm sorry. I completely forgot."

"Yeah, well, whatever." I started walking toward the counter. I couldn't believe I had let her get to me like that. I didn't need her. I didn't need anybody.

"No, no! Let me explain! It's important. See, I decided to go home for lunch today. And the mail came. I—"

"Oh God!" I shouted. I had just come around the counter. Jason was in a heap behind it.

I dropped to my knees and rolled him over to his back. He was gray, but he was still breathing. They were huge, rasping breaths.

"Jason! Jason, can you hear me?" I shouted in his face. "Oh, God, Jason! Jason!"

I looked around frantically. Kayla was peering over the counter with huge eyes. "Call 911!" I yelled, "Call 911 and tell them—"

"No," Jason coughed weakly. "It's all right."

I turned back to him wildly. His patch was skewed off his face, but his good eye was half-open. "All right? All right?" I demanded. "This is not all right!"

His right hand patted my arm weakly. "It is, though. I just—just took my meds—a little late, that's all."

"That's all? You collapse without a sound and that's all? I don't think so!" I turned back to Kayla. "Damnit, for once in your life will you actually do something? Call 911!"

"No," Jason repeated, but this time with more strength. He was looking past me, and I knew Kayla hadn't moved. "Don't call." He turned his eye back to me. "If you feel the need to do something, you could drive me home."

I just stared at him for a few long seconds. Then behind me, Kayla softly said, "Stet?" I turned around.

She was holding the phone handset and she lifted it in a silent question. I turned back to Jason. His eye had drifted closed again, but his color was better and his breathing was easy, almost like he was sleeping. Without turning back to her or saying anything, I shook my head.

"Thank you," Jason murmured without opening his eyes. "I'd hate to fire you for not following orders after all these years." He coughed weakly again. "Go ahead and close up. I'll just wait here."

"What needs to be done?" I asked him. "No one's been here for the last two hours."

"Oh. Yeah. Just make sure the register's locked, then. And get the lights."

"What do you want me to do?" Kayla asked.

"Go home," I said without looking at her as I secured the register.

"I'd like to help."

I didn't say anything as I reached past her and flipped off the lights. I went back to Jason. He had adjusted his eye patch and pushed himself up against the wall. I helped him the rest of the way to his feet, and then put one arm around his waist. "Ready?"

He nodded, and we began walking slowly around the counter.

"Go home, Kayla."

"I want to help," she repeated stubbornly. "The least I can do is shut the gate after you leave."

Jason stumbled a little, so I didn't answer her right

away. "How can I know you'll do it? Just because you say you will don't mean much."

Kayla got almost as pale as Jason had been. She lifted her chin, but she didn't say anything—to me.

"You really okay, Jason?"

"I'm fine, darlin'."

We were stepping out of the office door. Kayla pulled it shut behind us. Without saying anything, I reached back, opened it again, and turned the bottom knob, locking the door. Kayla crossed her arms over her chest.

I started to fish my keys out of my pocket. Jason handed me his keys instead.

"But Jason—" I began. Then I stopped. Of course he would want his car at his house. He might need it later.

Kayla spoke up. "I'll follow you in the Falcon."

"You're not old enough."

"So? I won't get pulled over."

"What if you do?"

"I'll tell them the truth. It's a medical emergency."

"Like they'll believe that," I said, looking pointedly at her skimpy shirt and short skirt.

"Stetson, I've had enough of your crap!"

"You ain't seen nothin' yet!" I retorted.

"Now, now," Jason mumbled, sounding like he was half-asleep. "You kids play nice."

I helped him the rest of the way to his car, and got him settled in the passenger seat. When I shut the door, I discovered Kayla standing defiantly by the Falcon. I walked over to her, stopping just inches away from her. She winced, like she expected a blow.

As I pulled my keys out of my pocket, I never took my

eyes off her. Slowly and clearly I said, "Drive it home. Park it in the shed. Lock the doors. That's it. Go anywhere else with it, and I'll kill you."

I expected argument. To my surprise, she merely nodded, took the keys, and got in the driver's seat. I watched as she pulled the door shut and then reached for the seat belt that wasn't there. She put the key in the ignition. The Falcon started smoothly and obediently. The lights flashed on and she pulled away, leaving me with a funny feeling in my stomach.

CHAPTER SIXTEEN

I CLIMBED in Jason's car. He had his head back, and I assumed he was dozing. I promised myself that if his breathing got all rattly again, I would go directly to the hospital, no matter what he said.

I pulled out of the yard. I shut and locked the gates as quickly as I could, leaving the car door open. When I returned, Jason seemed the same.

"Thanks, Stet."

"For what?"

"For helpin' me out."

"It ain't no favor, man. I'm still on the clock," I said.

He didn't rise to the bait. "You ought to take your car and get on out of here, while you still can."

"You still on that kick?" Every couple of months for the last three years, he'd been tying to get me to leave. I kept telling him I didn't have a place to go, but he kept asking. Maybe he thought I'd find a rich relative somewhere.

"I never got off this kick."

"I'll be outta here right after graduation. You don't have to try to get rid of me any faster than that."

He shook his head. "Get your car, and your sister, and get out. This town is poison. It'll suck the dreams right out of you."

"You're doin' all right. And we got lots of people livin' out in the 'burbs."

"Yeah, we got our 'burb class and we got our trailer class. You ever seen any of 'em switch?"

"You're in the middle. Ain't quite in the 'burbs, sure ain't in the trailers."

"I'm close to bein' run into the trailers. If I didn't get my government check each month and had to live just off the yard, I'd be in the trailers too."

I didn't say anything.

"You got talent. I think your sister does too. Don't let her become one of the trailer girls."

"We ain't got nowhere to go, Jason." I didn't put any emotion into my voice. "I'm almost eighteen and then I can go where I want. Kayla's just fourteen. She's got to have a guardian, and I'm not ready for that."

He snorted. "You know full well you're gonna be acting as her guardian anyway."

We pulled into his driveway. It was a sign of how tired he was when he didn't even try to open his own door. He just sat there and waited for me to come around to his side.

As I opened the door, I said, "Come on, Jason. Tell me what's goin' on."

"I'm dyin'," he said as I started to pull him out of the car.

I was so startled, I almost let him fall back in. Just in time, I managed to grab him.

"I said I'm dyin', I didn't say try to kill me," he grumbled.

"What do you mean, dyin'?"

"Maybe you are dumb enough to just stay here. What do you mean what do I mean? I'm dyin'. Ain't that plain enough?"

I just stood there and stared at him.

"Could we go inside now?" he demanded.

I stepped forward and put my arm around his waist again to help him into the house. Suddenly I was painfully aware of how much weight he had lost in the last few months. Why hadn't I noticed that before?

We went inside in silence. He pointed to the couch, and I steered him to it. He sat down, and took a couple of deep breaths.

"Thanks," he said. "You can take my car back to your house. Then come get me in the morning and take me to the yard before you go to school."

I shook my head. "You don't just tell me you're dyin' and then start talking about other crap. What's goin' on? What's wrong? What meds are you on?"

"Cancer. Got painkillers, and they said that's pretty much all they can do for me now."

"What about that chemo stuff? Or some kind of drugs? What about surgery, cuttin' out the tumor or whatever?"

"Ain't that kind of cancer, and it's gone too far."

"How long have you had it?"

"Who knows? I may have had it for years. The doc seems to think I've probably had it at least eight months, but he can't tell for sure."

"They really can't do anything?" In spite of my best efforts, my voice cracked.

"Nope."

I sat down on the floor and stared at the carpet. I wanted to cry. I wanted to yell. I wanted to find somebody to blame and kill them. I wanted to make Jason better. But all I did was sit there.

"You go on home and talk to Kayla. Maybe your mom

had a relative she knows, someone who could get you both out of here."

"I'm not leaving you."

"Stet, I'll be here in the morning," he said almost gently.

"I'm not leaving," I repeated stubbornly. "You may need some help tonight."

"And what are you gonna do tomorrow?"

"I'll—" I swallowed hard but plowed ahead. "I'll stay here with you."

"What about school? You said they'll kick you out if you miss any more, remember?"

"Yeah."

"You'd give up your high school diploma for me?"

I didn't look up. The carpet was fascinating.

"What about tomorrow night? And the next day? And the next?"

Now I did look up at him.

"Stet, I'm *dying*. You got your whole life. You got to move on."

"No, I got to spend time with you." I could feel the tears in my eyes now. "I'm not gonna have much more of that."

"No," he said. "You're not. You're fired, for one."

"What?"

"Well, maybe laid off is better. I'm selling the yard."

"Why?"

"I'm gonna go up to the Vet's Hospital. I'll check in. They'll take care of me until I check out."

"You're gonna give up just like that? Just quit?"

"I fight the fights I can win, Stet, You know that."

"Maybe you can win this one—" I began.

"Stet, I think I already have."

I shook my head. "How?"

He smiled in a strange way. "That's for later. Go on home. Come back tomorrow before school if you want."

"No. I'm staying here tonight. Caring for the ill and elderly is my new charity."

He glared at me. "You are one stubborn smart-ass."

"You taught me well."

He smiled again, but this time it was natural. "Yeah, I guess I did." He took a couple of deep breaths. I could tell he was in pain. "There's an envelope on the kitchen counter. Get it for me, will ya?"

I got up and found the envelope. I heard the TV come on. Before I went back out, I opened the fridge. "Want anything?"

"A soda would be good."

I grabbed two cans and headed back to the living room. As I handed him the envelope, I took the remote out of his hand.

"Hey!"

"Just because I'm stayin' here tonight don't mean I'm watchin' any of your crappy shows."

"Ha! You wouldn't know a good show if you saw one."

"I've seen plenty. In fact, I think I'll let you watch a few tonight."

Jason grumbled, but I just ignored him while I flipped through the channels. He pulled a piece of paper out of his pocket, unfolded it, and then opened the envelope.

"Yep, got it right."

"Got what right?" I asked, still watching the TV.

"Your VIN number."

"What?"

"Vehicle Identification Number. Don't you know—"

"I know what it is," I broke in. "Why do you need it?"

"To register the car, of course." He handed me the envelope. There were the registration papers and a temporary
license plate.

"Jason, I . . . " I was speechless.

"I know the car's worth more than what I put its value
at but I didn't want to pay more taxes. The plates'll be in
sometime next month."

"Why so long?" I asked.

"The new fancy plates take longer."

"You got me personalized plates?"

Jason grinned.

"I'm almost afraid to ask. What do they say?"

He just grinned even bigger.

"Jason? I'm the one who's gonna be drivin' around with
those tags, man. They'd better be cool."

"They are."

"So what are they?"

"Can't you read?"

I turned back to the papers in front of me. I scanned
them, and finally found a line that said, "The license plate
FREEHND has been placed in your name. It will . . ."

"Freehnd?" I tried.

"Free*hand*," Jason said. I just stared at him. "You
know, the way you do your artwork, freehand? And now
that you've got the car running you'll have a free hand? It's
gonna give you a free hand to do what you want?"

I was nodding slowly.

"That's cool enough, right?"

"Oh, yeah," I said, still stunned.

"You sure?" Jason asked, sounding worried. I looked up at him. "I mean, if you don't like it—"

"Jason, it's awesome! I just—I can't—thank you enough, man. Really. Thank you so much!"

He got a little red. "It ain't nothin'."

I knew better than to hug him, so I just said thank you another ten or twelve times.

We watched a few TV shows, or rather, I did. Jason dozed in and out for most of them. Finally, around ten, I convinced him to go to bed. I walked him down the hall to his room and over to his bed.

As he sat down, I asked, "You need anything else?"

"Nah," he said, shaking his head.

"You took your meds?"

He glowered at me with his good eye. "You don't need to baby me, Stet. There are a couple blankets in the hall closet. I think you'll find the couch comfortable enough."

"Now who's babying who?"

He just grunted at me. I laughed, and walked to the hall. When I got to his bedroom door, however, I stopped.

"You really gonna sell the yard?" I asked, looking back at him.

"Yeah." He looked up at me. "I thought about just makin' you the manager, or even givin' it to ya—"

"Jason, don't—"

"But I realized," he continued, "that if I did that, you'd stay. And you need to leave town. While your dreams are still alive."

●　●　●

I didn't sleep well that night. I must have called home

eight or nine times before I finally gave up. I wanted to talk to Kayla, apologize for what I had said, and ask her about the letter she had mentioned. Maybe she had found a way out.

Although I'd never admit it, I got up three times during the night just to check on Jason. Each time I went to his door, and then just stood there, listening for his breathing. One time he was snoring, and another time I heard him cough and roll over. The other time he was just breathing deeply, sound asleep. I wish I had been.

When six o'clock rolled around, I was wide awake. I decided I'd take Jason's car, go pick Kayla up and save her the walk to school. I jotted a quick note for Jason, left it on the kitchen table, and then checked on him once more. Snoring and out cold. Hopefully, he'd still be asleep when I got back.

As I was driving down Main Street, I was trying to decide if it would be worth my time to try to talk to Mr. Kincaid this morning. Maybe he would understand and get me excused for a few days to help Jason.

There was little traffic this early, but of course all of it was going my way. Although the sun wasn't up yet, the beginning light of dawn made it possible to see.

I passed MacGregor's. It was silent, but the still glowing neon signs seemed to mock me.

Suddenly I slammed on the brakes. The car behind me blared its horn and squealed its tires as it swerved to avoid me. I noticed, but barely. My whole being was focused on the skid marks leading to the mangled Falcon on the edge of the road.

Numbly, I pulled Jason's car over and then got out. I

took a few wobbly steps, and then had to stop and lean against his car.

The Falcon was totaled. The front end had rammed into a large tree, and the whole left side had collapsed. You couldn't see any of the Falcon's eyes or beak. The left front wheel stuck out at a cockeyed angle. In the windshield there were two stars, the bigger one on the driver's side. Both of them were bloodstained.

I couldn't even turn my head before I threw up. Fortunately my stomach was empty and it was mostly just dry heaves. Spots floated before my eyes. I closed them tightly, hoping to erase the image in front of me. When I opened them again, though, the young bird was still there, still broken.

Somehow I managed to get back in Jason's car. I started the engine, and tried to think. Where did I go from here? Would anyone be a home? Should I go directly to the hospital?

I put the car in gear and just let it kind of drive itself home. I was almost there anyway, I thought. I might as well check there first.

Pulling up, I saw John Stevens's truck. Inside, the lights were on.

Slowly I climbed the three steps to the front door. I opened it and stopped just inside. Dad was sitting on the couch, his head bandaged and his left leg in a cast, propped up on a pillow.

"What happened?" I asked in confusion.

"There was an accident last night," John said. He was standing behind the kitchen counter, stirring coffee.

"Who was in it?" I came in and stood at the end of the

counter. A notebook lay open with pages of loopy handwriting. Kayla had been doing homework.

"Your dad and Kayla."

"Why didn't anyone call me?"

"We just got here," John answered. "Things were kind of crazy at the hospital."

"Where's Kayla?" I asked.

Dad was staring at his toes poking out of the cast.

"He's sedated," John said.

"Were you there?" I asked John.

He shook his head. "Not really."

I raised my eyebrows, but turned to my father. "What happened, Dad?"

He raised his hands in a helpless gesture and shook his head.

"He got fired yesterday," John said in a low voice. "He went straight to MacGregor's and started drinking. Right before closing, I found him in a back booth, passed out."

Dad kind of moaned and held his hand up to his head.

"I got him to come to, sort of, and asked if he wanted a ride home. He said he'd get one. Said he didn't want to ride with a slave driver."

John must have been the one who gave Dad his notice.

"What happened, Dad?" I asked again.

"I called you for a ride," he said sullenly.

"I wasn't here."

"Kayla was. I told her to come get me."

The shock I had been feeling was slowly being replaced with rage. "And she agreed?"

"No. She said she couldn't drive. Some crap about it bein' your car and no license or somethin'. She actually hung up on me!" Even through the drugs, the rage at this memory came through. "I called her back and told her to come get me or get her ass out of my trailer."

For the second time that morning I closed my eyes in an attempt to erase what was there.

"So she came to get you."

"Yep. But she wouldn't let me drive. Said she was afraid I'd hit something." He snorted.

"You were blind drunk," John said from the counter. "It was a good decision at the time."

I looked at him. "What do you mean?"

John just stared at Dad, so I looked at Dad too. "What happened?" I practically shouted.

"A deer."

"A deer?"

"A deer jumped out in the road. She swerved to avoid it and ran us right into that old elm." He looked up at me, his drugged eyes clearing just a little. "She was tellin' me somethin' about Caroline. But I didn't understand her. I don't know any Caroline. Do you?"

"No," I said, shaking my head.

"That's all she would talk about. Caroline. The last thing she said . . ." Dad's voice trailed off.

"What? What did you just say?"

"Caroline, something about—"

"No! No, damnit! What did you say about her last words?" I turned frantically to John. His eyes were sad. "Isn't she at the hospital? Shouldn't someone be with her?"

Slowly he began shaking his head. "She won't know you're there."

"What do you mean?" I asked John.

Dad kept prattling on. "Dumb girl wouldn't move till I had my seat belt on. Then she never put hers on."

"John?"

"Flight for Life had to come."

Again the dry heaves washed over me. I fell to my knees.

John came around the corner and put his hands on my shoulders. "Take it easy, son. Take it easy."

"Kayla," I croaked.

"She was pretty messed up. But she still might make it."

"Where—"

"They were gonna take her to Children's Hospital, where they've got a lot of specialists."

"For what?"

"They wouldn't tell me anything else. I'm not family."

I turned back to Dad. "What happened?" I asked again. "What kind of specialist does she need?"

Dad was staring vacantly at the dark TV. "He's still doped up," John said again. "Maybe later he'll remember what they told him."

"I'm sorry about your car, Stetson," Dad said from the couch. "It was supposed to be a bird, right?"

I stared at him in disbelief for a second and then I launched myself at him. "You bastard! How dare you do this to us! How dare you treat her like that!—" I went on, ranting and swearing. I wanted to tear him limb from limb for all he hadn't done. John caught me before I got to the sofa, though, and held my arms behind my back.

"Get out!" Dad suddenly roared. Sedated or not, I had finally broken through. "Get out of my house! Take your lousy stuff and get the hell out! I don't need to take your crap! I kept you around and your mom never come back! Then she dies and leaves me with another brat! You two ain't been nothin' but trouble! Both think you're too good for me, too good to hang out with me."

Tears were streaming down my face. "I'll get out!" I shouted back. "I'll get out and you won't know what to do! You can't find the grocery store or the washing machine! You don't know when the bills are due! I'll get out and you'll be kicked out before the month's over!"

I wrenched myself out of John's strong grip and bolted for my room. I ripped the pillows out of their cases and began stuffing my clothes inside.

"Stet," John said from the door, "I don't think this is a good idea."

"It's a great idea," I said, trying to see through the tears in my eyes. "It's the best idea the old fool has ever had."

"He's not himself. He's in shock, drugged—"

"Yeah, he's not himself. He's a lot nicer right now."

"Stet—"

"He can't stop me. I'm leaving." I turned to leave when something on my desk caught my eye. An open envelope, addressed to Kayla. The return address was in Kansas. I grabbed it and stuck it in my back pocket.

John was standing in the door, his big body practically filling the whole frame. I stopped right in front of him, holding both pillowcases, not saying a word. His mouth twisted in a sad little frown, and he stepped aside. I walked past him, and didn't turn my head as I went through the living room and then out the door.

CHAPTER SEVENTEEN

I PULLED into Jason's driveway, turned off the car, and just sat there. I had too many emotions inside that I wasn't used to.

How could I care so much? She had only been in my life for a week. And it hadn't been a very good week at that. She was in serious condition, yeah, but she had also totaled my car, my life. Still the tears kept coming. I couldn't make them stop.

Leaning my head back against the headrest, I closed my eyes. I needed to go in and see how Jason was doing. Me, I felt like I had just been hit by an eighteen wheeler.

I moved just a little and heard a crinkling. The envelope. I reached back and pulled it out of my pocket. There were three pieces of paper in it. Two of them were stationery, and the name Caroline was signed at the bottom of the second one. The other one was a piece of notebook paper, and it was only half full.

My dear Kayla,

Of course I remember you! However, I will admit I was a little surprised to hear from you. You were only a little girl the last time I saw you.

I was so sorry to hear about your mother. And I'm sorry that your reunion with your father hasn't been as smooth as it could have been. It would have helped, I'm sure, if you had at least known him before going to live with him.

I knew your father before he married your mother. He was a reckless bull-rider and never did anything halfway, until he had to quit. The situation you describe does not surprise me, but I'm not sure I can give you the answer you would like.

I would love to have you come stay for an extended visit. Becoming your guardian is something we would have to discuss later. You may not like me either, after all. And I do have four children of my own. Our house would be crowded.

And the invitation is open for Stetson, too, if he would like to meet his mother's family. I remember how much your mother cried when she left him. The doctors were concerned that it might affect your health! But she knew if she brought Stetson, your father would never leave her alone. He loved Stetson too much to ever let him go.

Well, this is enough rambling for now, I am sure. I would love to see both of you, my dear, and spend time catching up. Please let me know when I can expect to see you.

> *Affectionately,*
> *Caroline*

Her phone number was printed neatly at the bottom.

I had to reread the letter twice. My father loved me too much to ever let me go? Where had she gotten that idea? And if my mother had really cried that much, why hadn't she ever come back for me? Or called? Or written?

Then I turned to Kayla's letter.

Dear Aunt Caroline,
Thank you so much for the letter! It helps a

*whole lot to know that I have somewhere I can
go, even if it's only for a little while. Things here
are still bad, but at least now I can talk to Stet.
I'm starting school*

There the big loopy writing stopped. I wondered if it
would ever be finished.

I saw the curtain shift in the window. Jason was up.
Slowly I got out of the car and walked to his front door. I
needed his help.

● ● ●

I don't remember much of my last three days in town. I
did drop by school to see Mr. Kincaid. I asked how to
transfer schools. Then I got the information on the GED
program, and asked if it would matter if I tried to take it
in Kansas instead.

"You can take it anywhere. I'm glad you're considering
it."

"I still want my diploma," I said. "This is just in case."

"I understand. I thought Kayla was doing better."

"She is." And that was true, sort of. When I had gone
to visit her, she still hadn't come out of the coma, but she
had stabilized enough to be transferred to Kansas. That
happened to be the closest pediatric specialist. They
thought that she might regain consciousness in the next
week. I hoped so. Sitting with her when she was silent and
strapped to all those machines was freaky.

"But you're going to stay in Kansas?"

"That's my plan."

"What's in Kansas, Stet?" he asked as I started to leave.

"I'm not sure yet."

"So why go?"

"'Cause it's a chance. And I don't have one here."

Mr. Kincaid didn't have anything to say to that. He just nodded and wished me luck.

I called Aunt Caroline. It was one of the hardest things I had ever done. Not only did it bug me to make a long-distance call on Jason's bill, but I had to talk to a stranger about personal stuff. My voice broke several times as I told her about Kayla, and I almost had to hang up. But I kept it together long enough to get directions and let her know my plans. She asked to talk to Jason, and said she'd call my father.

Although I didn't want to, I had to go back to the trailer for a couple more things. I opened the front door and headed straight through the living room.

In my room, I quickly scooped up my other pair of shoes, and last couple of shirts. Then I tossed Kayla's clothes into her two suitcases. Waiting at Jason's was the shirt I had done for her. It was a knight in shining armor, complete with sword and lance, but instead of a horse, he was riding a falcon.

I turned around slowly in my room, surprised by its starkness. All I had gathered were clothes, and yet you'd never know I had lived there. As I walked back toward the front door, I hoped I would be able to forget my presence as quickly as it had.

"Just put it back."

I bit back a yelp as I spun around. I had forgotten that Dad was laid up and out of a job.

He was sitting in the dark corner of the living room.

"Put it back and just forget about it."

"Forget about what?"

He waved his hand in the air. "Everything."

"I can't."

"You mean you won't."

I just met his stare. He was looking old, and tired, smaller somehow.

"You got to stay. How else you gonna graduate?"

"That's none of your business."

"I'm your father—"

"You're an ignorant drunk."

Anger flashed across his face, but was quickly gone. "It eases the pain."

"You could have talked to me. You just love drinking and being at MacGregor's more."

"You remind me of her too much."

"What?"

"Every year, you look more like her, act more like her. I can't—couldn't stand it. I can do better now."

"I doubt it."

"Come on, let's have a beer."

"I'm leaving."

"Stetson, you need me."

"No, Dad, I don't. *You* need *me.*"

I was reaching for the doorknob when he said, "You're right." If he had said anything else, I would have been out the door. But that stopped me cold.

"Stay, Stet. Please."

I leaned my head against the door. "I can't. If I don't go now, I'll never leave."

"Is that such a bad thing?"

"Yeah. I think it is." I reached in my pocket and pulled out Caroline's phone number. I copied it and tore off the corner, setting it on the bookshelf. "Here. If you ever sober up, give me a call."

● ● ●

Jason sold the salvage yard to Nick Arnot, but not before the Falcon got towed back to it.

Aside from when I first told him what had happened to Kayla, we didn't talk much. He was dealing with his pain, and I was dealing with the confused disaster my life had become. After our last day at the yard, I drove him back to his house.

"Can I ask a favor, Stet?"

"Sure," I said tiredly. I had been tired for too long.

"I need to go to the hospital tomorrow," he began.

"I know. I'll take you."

He nodded, as if he expected that, but then continued, "I'll be staying for a while, so—"

"I'll leave tomorrow," I said. "I know you need to sell the house." I opened the refrigerator and stared at the cans for a long moment. Finally I pulled out a soda and opened it.

He nodded again, sadly. I thought he was gonna say something else, but he just shuffled slowly down the hall to his room.

The next morning was foggy. I drove slowly through the town, knowing I wouldn't see it again for a long time. The drive was awkward for me. I wanted to talk to Jason, but I didn't know what to say. I hated to leave him, but I couldn't wait to go.

"Just drive up to the patient drop-off," Jason directed as I made the last turn for the hospital.

"You mean patient parking, don't you?"

"No, patient drop-off. It'll be easier."

"Okay," I said, sighing. It would mean I'd have to go park the car and then take the keys in to him later. I had been hoping to avoid going into the hospital. I didn't want to see him there.

I pulled into the front drive. Jason started to get out, but he was moving slowly, and I was out of the car and holding the door open for him before he had his feet on the ground. I shut the door and he leaned against the car while I got his two small bags out of the back.

I had shipped Kayla's bags, but I still had my pillowcases of clothes, and the air compressor. The letters were both in my back pocket. Again I wondered how I was going to get everything, especially the heavy compressor, to Kansas. I couldn't afford a bus ticket so I was going to have to hitch, but I knew a lot of time would be spent walking. I shut the trunk and walked back to the front of the car.

An orderly had arrived with a wheelchair and was trying to get Jason to sit down in it.

"No," he said, shaking his head. "I'm goin' in on my own two feet."

"Here," I said, putting his bags on the chair. "Push the chair in."

The orderly and I exchanged looks as Jason started pushing the wheelchair inside. I shrugged. Jason didn't realize that the chair was acting like a walker.

I turned to follow him.

"Gotta move the car," the orderly said. "Can't leave it here."

I groaned. Jason stopped and turned around. "Go on," I said. "I'll find you inside."

Jason left the wheelchair and walked shakily back to me. "No. You go on."

"I gotta bring your keys back."

"Nah," he said, shaking his head. "Take the car."

"What?"

"I can't use it while I'm here. All it will do is sit in the lot. You call me when you get to Kansas and give me your number. When I'm ready to leave, I'll call you. You can come get me."

We both knew I wouldn't be coming back to get him. Swallowing the lump in my throat I said, "What makes you think I'll come all the way back from Kansas just for you?"

He smiled but didn't answer. He didn't have to.

"Take care of yourself, Stet," he said, holding out his hand.

I brushed past his hand and hugged him tight for the first time in all the years I knew him.

He clapped me soundly on the back a couple of times, then stepped back. We were both blinking a little too much.

"You call me."

"I will," I promised.

"Now go on. Go visit your sister and then meet your aunt."

I nodded, but still couldn't seem to move.

This time it was Jason who stepped forward for the hug. "You'll be okay, Stet," he whispered fiercely. "You'll be just fine."

Then he turned his back on me.

I walked around to the car, and as I opened the door, I saw the orderly helping Jason into the wheelchair. I watched as they disappeared inside, but Jason didn't turn around. Just as I was going to get in, he suddenly stuck his hand out to the side, flipping me off.

I drove slowly down the hospital driveway. Caroline was taking us in, at least until we each graduated. She had even talked my father into signing power of attorney papers over to her. Her only stipulation was that I do school full-time, no jobs. That suited me just fine. I needed to be in class next week.

As I pulled onto the highway, I was grateful for the fog. I had a long drive in front of me, and if I could have seen the whole road, I might not have had the courage to start.